IRVING STONE

False Witness

A NOVEL

NEW YORK

The Book League of America

1940

PRINTED AT THE *Country Life Press*, GARDEN CITY, N. Y., U. S. A.

7

To

MAURICE BERKSON

(*not only because we love him*)

FALSE WITNESS

THE CAR MOVED SLOWLY along the concrete highway that cut the little valley in half.

"How beautiful it is," murmured the driver, gazing at the vivid green alfalfa fields and the orange groves hung with honey-colored fruit. "What a marvelous sense of peace and security a man could enjoy in a secluded spot like this."

His companion was silent for a moment, remembering.

"When I was a young boy we had a storm here that came close to wrecking this valley and the happiness of most of the people in it. When we cross the bridge you'll be able to see Mission Oaks; if not for the love and courage of an eighteen-year-old girl, Margaret Annister, this prosperous community might have become just another of California's ghost towns."

UNTIL THE DAY the Widow Smithers' money disappeared, Mission Valley was a peaceful community of five hundred souls; but for no one was it more friendly than for John Annister. As he sat in his front yard under one of a ring of seven giant oaks he could see before him the saucer floor of the valley, every acre broken to the plow. When he had first climbed the Pacific Ocean flank of the Santa Monica mountains and gazed in reverential awe at this former lake bottom, with the San Felice River tumbling in through the north pass of the Sierra Madre range opposite, it had been as untouched as when Cabrillo had led an expedition up the same Indian trail and cast the first pair of white man's eyes upon a California valley.

False Witness

Where only thirty-seven years before John Annister had watched herds of deer and antelope grazing among the wild mustard and tule, he could now see the village of San Felice, trim and white in the early spring sunlight. Everything had grown fast: the crops, the houses, the tiny town they had staked out in the central barley field of the five-mile circular valley. The young men had married and had children, and their children had had children. In time he too had married and had a child, and his child had had a child. It was her voice he was waiting for now as he drowsed on a hand-hewn wooden bench after a five-hour stretch behind the plow, a sinewy New Englander, just a quarter of an inch under six feet, with lean gray hair contoured close to the head, weather-parched skin, a close-clipped white mustache, twinkling blue eyes and powerful lean hands gnarled from thirty-seven years of grappling with the earth. Though his next birthday would be his sixtieth, there were few young men in the neighborhood who could force down his arm at Indian wrestling: it had long been a saying in Mission Valley that John Annister was as hard of body as he was soft of spirit.

He looked up with a slow smile to watch his granddaughter Margaret come toward him. She had begun putting up her hair the Christmas before, and it still surprised him to see how mature she looked at seventeen. His neighbors, recognizing Margaret's lithe figure, the close-fitting hair pulled back sharply from the rounded brow, the lucid blue eyes, all said she was the spit and image of her grandfather. From the kindness and twinkle in her eye they imagined her to be soft and easygoing, but John had very early discovered the subterranean channels of passionate strength.

"They didn't know her grandmother," he thought, "or they would remember that deep black hair and the small mouth. We never had those in the Annister family."

"I've set the table under the patio oak, Gramp."

"Ah, good. It's three months now since we were able to eat out of doors."

"This is the first day it's been warm enough, the first day of spring, really."

For a moment, before rising, he listened to her voice, gentle and low-pitched, full of music; the rich tonal qualities came as a fresh pleasantness even to those who knew her best. Margaret had never been fond of talk for its own sake; John had observed that she was one to plow her convictions deep before planting words in them.

False Witness

"Come, lazybones. Mary Shoe was filling the tureen when I left the kitchen."

Margaret had spread his favorite red-and-white-checked cloth over the split log table they had built together three years before when the old one had collapsed. While they sat side by side, waiting for Grace Rogers to come out of the house, they could watch the freshets of the San Felice River flow over the fieldstone dam.

"Where is your mother?"

"I've called her twice. Mary, is Mother on her way out?"

Mary Shoemaker set down the covered tureen before glancing dubiously toward the west wing.

"Now that's something hard to tell, Miss Margaret."

John had lifted the cover of the tureen and was sniffing its savory contents.

"Lord love me," he murmured, "duck and dumplings on the first day of every spring. It was nice of you to remember, Mary."

"I did the cooking, Mr John," she replied; "it was Miss Margaret did the remembering."

She was a ponderous, slow-moving widow of forty-four. Left childless and penniless when her husband was killed in an explosion, Mary Shoemaker had become the valley handy woman, going into the farmers' homes to cook for parties, sew new dresses or bed-spreads, nurse the sick. On Tuesdays and Fridays she came to the Annisters to bake them a supply of bread and pie, to scrub the floors and do whatever mending was necessary. She worked her way and asked no favors; for this attitude, though she occupied the lowest position in the vaguely demarcated Mission Valley social structure, she was respected wherever she went.

"I'll go call Mrs Rogers again," she said.

John and Margaret were halfway through their dinner before Grace Rogers came down the porch steps to join them under the oak.

"You might have waited for me," she said querulously.

"We called you three times, Mother," replied Margaret quietly. "You know Gramp doesn't enjoy his duck and dumplings unless they're burning hot."

"Well, just the same," said Grace. She helped herself liberally from the bowl Mary had uncovered for her. "Mary, don't forget to wash the dinner dishes before you leave."

John and Margaret exchanged a quick glance that had in it more of annoyance than amusement.

"Grace, it's a full fifteen years now that Mary has

been helping out in our house. Can you ever remember the time she went off and left the dishes?"

"Well, just the same."

While John ate the apple pie Mary had set before him he mused, as he so often did, at the differences between mother and daughter. His perplexity was even greater than it had been at the differences between himself and his daughter when he had been young and it had mattered deeply.

Lighting his battered old pipe, he walked toward the dam and sat on the bank with his face to the sun. With the nostalgia of these first warm fragrant hours of spring his mind went back to that April day in 1866 when he had descended the trail on the valley side of the Santa Monica hills, making toward this dam in the river. What was a stone dam doing in a valley where there was no visible life except bear and coyote and coveys of dove and quail? While crossing the dam he had perceived from its vantage point some half-covered foundations in a nearly perfect circle of giant oaks. Dropping his army haversack onto the ledge, he had excitedly examined the foundations, unearthing a complete rectangular building base.

He had spent the rest of the day reconnoitering from the dam, but always he had come back to the ring of seven oaks, each with a spread that would have covered his parents' farmhouse in New Hampshire. That night he had built a fire under the oak nearest the Indian trail, had cooked his flapjacks, bacon and coffee, spread his army blanket and lay looking up at the stars. For the first time in his three-thousand-mile journey, for the first time since he had been eighteen and had answered Abe Lincoln's call to preserve the crumbling Union, he felt a gentle peace envelop him. He had known that whatever else there might be in this wide new world, he had at last found his home place: here, a man would walk in beauty no matter which way he set his steps.

When dawn began prodding loose the blackness of the Sierra Madres opposite, and the eastern stars were covered with a pale rose light, he slung his haversack onto his back and tramped along the bank of the river to the south pass where the Santa Monica and Sierra Madre ranges curved and tumbled down to touch each other's toes. It was mid-afternoon before he covered the twenty miles into Los Angeles, a sprawling sun-baked Mexican settlement of adobe houses and enormous land-grant haciendas. At the county assessor's office he learned that Phineas Lancaster owned the entire valley, his father having bought it for eleven cents an acre from Pio Pico, who had needed money to repulse the Americanos under Fremont. From black-bearded Phineas, who welcomed the boy into his study, John also learned that Franciscan friars had built a mission inside the ring of seven oaks at the end of the eighteenth century, when the valley had been part of the route of the Mexican army journeying between San Diego and Monterey. Though a raging flood of the San Felice River had washed away the adobe walls, the country had ever since been known as Mission Valley.

John Annister had bought ten acres on either side of the dam for twenty-five dollars an acre, paying with a United States government check.

"See here, my boy," said Phineas, "is this five-hundred-dollar check all the money you have?"

"Yes sir."

"Then you'd better keep a hundred of it for tools and seed. You can pay me back out of your first crop. No, no thanks, please. I like to see young men settle out here; it means we'll have a chance to make something of this new state."

All that spring, summer and fall John Annister had worked from dawn to dark, clearing, plowing, planting, reaping. The hot valley sun had healed his bullet wounds, poured back into him the young strength he had squandered in three years of cold and muddy trenches. From his first crop of barley he had earned enough to pay half his debt, to buy peach, apricot and orange trees to plant in the rich loam alongside the river.

He had already begun to feel the first twinges of loneliness when, at the Christmas dinner to which he had been invited by Phineas Lancaster, he had met Margarita Abila, daughter of one of the first Spanish settlers and rulers of California. For the first few moments they spoke together John had wondered what it was her voice reminded him of; then he had remembered: the low music of water tinkling over the dam by the mission oaks while he lay on the bank wrapped in his army blanket. The music of the water flowing over the dam this opening day of spring sent his mind back to the exquisitely fragile Margarita of the deep black hair parted in the center and combed round to conceal the ears, of the two tiny pearl earrings to match her white teeth, of the big black eyes so widely spaced in so slender an oval, smoldering eyes that were withal honest, strong.

If John had once managed to tear his gaze from the lovely Spanish girl, he would have seen Phineas Lancaster smiling to himself as he stroked his bushy side whiskers. Before the Christmas dinner was over John knew he had found the inevitable mistress for his mission oaks. Margarita was the symbol of everything he had yearned and searched for in his long journey across the land: hot sun, vibrant color, deep music, inner peace, loyalty that would keep them together all the days of their life.

They were married three weeks later in Lancaster's spacious drawing room, then drove through the south pass to Mission Oaks—as they had decided to call their farm—in John's wagon, laden with his bride's many trunks of fine Spanish linens and laces, heavy silverware, hand-woven blankets, books and manuscripts and paintings she had inherited from her father. Utilizing the old mission foundations, Margarita had designed a rambling Mexican ranch house enclosing what was now the patio oak. In the cool weather that winter they had ridden horseback through the hills; in the heat of the summer they had bathed at the dam. During the long evenings she had played the piano in the private sitting room they had built for her music and books, singing to him Spanish love ballads in her low, tinkling voice.

The following summer a daughter had been born to

them, named Grace after John's grandmother. He had not been too disappointed, for the next year, he knew, would bring him a son. The second child had been a boy, a boy far too big for Margarita's delicate body; and John had lost them both.

If Grace had been another Margarita his sorrow might have been assuaged, but as the child grew up, dull in body and spirit, he came to feel his loss to be irretrievable. A man with a gentle nature, John Annister poured out his love on Mission Valley. When other war-weary veterans from the North and South alike, Europeans in search of gold and freedom, Midwesterners who felt cramped in the country their parents had pioneered, came over the trail from Santa Monica, John offered them hospitality in his big, empty house, showed them how this lake bottom should be plowed and planted, helped them build their houses and barns, roads and ditches. When his neighbors met hardship he staked them over the bad times, loaned them money to pay their debts or buy their land. As the oldest settler, people came to him not only to help shoulder their burdens, but to compromise their minor disputes. For his years of kindness Mission Valley paid John the highest compliment it could bestow: they said he loved good for its own sake.

Though he had never grown rich, he had bought the adjoining twenty acres from Phineas Lancaster, employed two of his neighbors' sons as hired men and generally managed to keep a couple of thousand dollars in the bank against a poor season.

When his daughter Grace was nineteen, a man by the name of Rogers drifted into the valley. John had hired him. Rogers was a secretive fellow but proved to be a conscientious worker. John had been delighted when Grace awakened from her lethargy long enough to fall in love with Rogers and marry him. At the end of twenty months she had given birth to a daughter; she had refused her father's plea that the girl be called Margarita, saying it was too foreign sounding for these modern times, but had finally made John happy by compromising on Margaret. When Margaret was only sixteen days old, and John had seen that first bright sparkle in her blue eyes, he realized he had been too hasty in thinking his loss to be irreparable. Time had merely skipped a generation.

For her fifth birthday he presented his granddaughter with his mare's first colt, and soon they became an increasingly familiar sight as together they rode the valley and foothills, the grandfather relating to the child the personal story of every road, clearing and furrow they passed. Since she was five Margaret could remember her love for the home place; the same qualities that had led John Annister to cherish this country were in her, intensified by Margarita's vibrantly alive, sensitive nature. It was not many years before she was warming John's heart by pointing out to him a subtle harmony of line or color his masculine eyes had missed.

He was still pulling ruminatively on his pipe when Mary Shoemaker came out of the kitchen with a knitted shawl over her shoulders. John walked back to the table under the oak.

"On your way home now, Mary?"

"No, Mr John, I'm going to the Widow Smithers. She's crippled up again with rheumatism."

"It's nice of you to help her."

Mary made some fragmentary answer behind her eyes, no part of which was uttered.

"I'll be back on Friday, then," she said. "Miss Margaret, those gingerbreads for the church supper to-morrow night are cooling on the window ledge."

As he watched Mary walk slowly along the river path toward the road, John quoted softly to his grand-daughter, " 'And the halt shall lead the lame.' " He rubbed the thumb and index finger of his left hand against the gray patch of beard on either side of his chin, as he so frequently did when something pleasured or pained him. "The second poorest woman in the valley is going to the poorest woman to help her with her work."

2

LATE THE FOLLOWING AFTERNOON, when he came in from plowing his alfalfa fields into rich black horizontals, his denim shirt and overalls stiff with sweat from the unseasonal heat, he found Margaret waiting for him at the dam in her knee-length bathing suit with the puffed shoulders.

"The sun has warmed the water, Gramp. A swim will refresh you for the social tonight."

He dressed on the far side of the river, where heavy oak branches reached to the ground to form a complete enclosure. Then they dove together from the ledge and swam across the river and back, their strokes matched. From the time Margaret had been a year old and her father, ostensibly going into Los Angeles on a business trip, had disappeared into as mysterious a future as the past from which he had emerged, John Annister had taken his granddaughter with him to the dam at the end of summer days to bathe her and later to teach her to swim by his side.

When they had dried themselves on heavy towels and returned to the house, John donned the white shirt, stand-up collar and starched cuffs Margaret had laid out on his bed, tied the wide black bow tie around the collar, wrestled his studs into place at the bosom, then put on his second-best suit, the heavy dark woolen with the lapeled vest that he wore in warm weather and cold alike. Margaret was already standing on the high-roofed Mexican porch, her creamy skin glowing from the swim, her hair glistening black as it lay coiled low on her slender neck. She had little patience with the bustles, bell flares and rufflings with which the stylists of 1903 adorned women's clothing; her new brown suit of percale had been severely tailored to lie flat and long, accentuating the stripling effect of her figure.

"How nice you look, child. Norman would like that suit."

Her eyes met his, clear, but with a matching twinkle; it was no secret that she and Norman Martell loved each other.

"He'll be here on Saturday, Gramp," she replied quietly.

"Isn't your mother coming to the social?"

"No. She has a headache."

They swung out along the hard-packed adobe road that had been widened by usage from the original Indian trail. The sun, setting behind the voluptuously curved Santa Monica hills, filled the valley with soft shell-pink light. A quarter of a mile to the west, the road ended in the clump of black walnut trees that surrounded the minister's cottage, and the trail to the church began. It was a white frame building with a fragile steeple in which was hung the deep-toned mission bell John had unearthed while digging for his house. John rarely failed to chuckle when he climbed the trail and realized afresh that he had brought to the California valley one of the churches of his White Mountains of New Hampshire.

It was pleasant for him to remember the night twenty-five years before when, at his summons, a dozen of the valley ranchers had gathered around his dining table to discuss the need, now that their children were growing up, of a church for the community. Five different creeds had been represented at that meeting, but since the families had barely enough money to build and maintain one church, they had decided to worship together. A service had been worked out: they would open with the invocation, they would sing a hymn, the minister would elaborate on a text from the Bible, they would sing another hymn, repeat the Lord's Prayer and receive the benediction: a ritual that could satisfy a simple Christian soul yet give offense to no one. At first there had been conflict of opinion, but the men had found it difficult not to compromise with neighbors who had helped in times of emergency to dig their irrigation ditches and gather their crops, whose wives had nursed their wives when their children had been born.

It was a long pull up the trail to the church; of a summer morning it could be burning hot, of a winter morning the rain from the Pacific could slash across the hillside; but the congregation had wanted their church above the floor of the valley and above the routine of ordinary living. Flood might wash out a crop, insects destroy it; trouble might come to a family, even sickness and death; but always, when they looked up, the trim white church stood above them, benign and unchanging. It was good to exert one's self a little on the trail before commending one's self to God.

Margaret and John continued their walk upward and were soon standing before the church, a simple house of worship as austere as the ritual upon which it had been based. From long habit John glanced up at the plaque embedded in the front beam, where everyone entering must see it. It was a wooden plaque with the Ninth Commandment burned into it by the Annister pyrographic needle, a small plaque, but the rock upon which the Union Church of Mission Valley had been founded. It read: THOU SHALT NOT BEAR FALSE WITNESS AGAINST THY NEIGHBOR. The plaque had been the only treasure John had carried with him from New Hampshire; his mother, at the last moment before kissing him good-by, had taken it off the wall of the Annister parlor and put it in his haversack.

He had had little trouble convincing the newly formed church board that gossip was the poison that could undermine their community; that, in order to make one church meet all the problems and serve all the religious forms that were bound to appear in the valley as the years went on, they would have to guard their unity as their most valued possession. At first there had been transgression, but the menfolk had remained firm, and the habit of idle talk about one's neighbors had never developed. After a year or two the women had found that even at their Tuesday coffee club, where there was little to do but embroider and make conversation, they could pass a pleasant afternoon without bearing witness against their neighbors. Mrs Hamil, the congenital talker who ordinarily would have served as the town tattler, contented herself by devouring the new novels and magazine serials as they appeared, retelling the fiction tales from house to house throughout the valley.

The rose colors were deepening to lavender when John and his granddaughter entered the community house that had been added to the north wall of the church to accommodate the growing social needs of the valley. Its one room was of unpainted pine, which gave it a rude but homey effect. While Margaret went to the kitchen in the rear to cut the gingerbread, John stood in the doorway enjoying the activity, smiling to the men who were carrying in heavy trays of food for their wives. Working with gusto at the serving table just in front of the kitchen were the womenfolk of the coffee club, their hair wound intricately on top of their heads, bravely wearing only tea aprons over their silk party dresses.

False Witness

Mrs Beaudry, whose family had come from South Carolina, was frying the most delicious chicken on the Pacific Coast. Mrs O'Melvany, whose baked hams spiced with quince melted on the foreground of one's tongue, was garnishing her masterpieces with parsley and sliced orange. Mrs Sepulveda's Spanish mother had passed on to her the secret of making enchiladas so peppery hot and yet so delicate they could not offend even a dyspeptic digestion. Mrs Wolkskill was stirring a cauldron of the Hungarian goulash that made her beloved of every family in the valley, and little Mrs Renaldi, who had no other social virtues, was adding grated cheese to the spaghetti that would be talked about until the first Wednesday of the next month. Mrs Neill mixed her bowl of green salad that had been cut from her vegetable garden while she laughed and talked with Mrs Atkinson, who was setting out her creamy potato salad. Mrs Jennifer unpacked the slabs of pale butter she had churned that afternoon to place them alongside Mrs Celis' trays of French bread, while Mrs Clauves, with her three-layer chocolate cakes, and Mrs Temple, with her cans of butter cookies, waved to Mrs Pupke to join them at the far end of the table with her mixers of strawberry ice cream.

As John watched he remembered what their first

minister, Jonathan Waite, had told him at the first of these church suppers:

"People who eat each other's good food remain friends."

He stepped out onto the porch of the community house; the sky stretched like a taut blue tarpaulin between the two mountain ranges. From where John stood he could see below him dim lights moving slowly along the roads, flickering lamps on the buggies that were converging on the clump of black walnuts. Like a veteran harbor master he could tell by its position in the valley to whose family each moving light belonged.

A heavy hand was laid upon his shoulder; he turned about to find Maxwell Widney, their new minister, grinning at him. Widney was twenty-five, a vitalic and genial six-footer with a blond cowlick that dangled over his forehead and tiny tan moles that stood out sharply from the light skin whenever he smiled or scowled. Night and day he could be found dashing about the valley on his bicycle, doing good works, coaching a baseball or soccer team, organizing a taffy pull or a magic-lantern show. If to the parishioners he had at first appeared a mite more physical than spiritual, they had soon decided that that was sinning on the proper side. After twenty-five years of Jonathan Waite, the last thing they could have stomached from a minister was unction.

"Magnificent night, isn't it?" he asked, shaking hands with John. "I'm going to tramp down to the ocean when the meeting is over. Could I persuade you to join me?"

"I have to plow my orange orchard in the morning, young man; that'll furnish me about all the exercise I can handle."

"They tell me you're still the valley champion at Indian wrestling; sometime, after you've had an exhausting day's work, I'm coming over to tackle you."

John's left thumb and index finger caressed the beard patch on either side of his chin.

"Here comes August Hauser; he's the only man in the congregation your size. Why don't you take him on?"

The minister looked dubious.

"I doubt whether Mr Hauser cares much about wrestling."

They stood watching August Hauser, the valley's justice of the peace and president of the church board, come puffing up the last few steps of the trail, mopping his red face with his handkerchief. At the time he had come to John Annister's, twenty-five years before, to form this church he had been a small farmer, trader and moneylender; now he was the richest man in Mission Valley, selling most of its produce in Los Angeles, controlling many acres through mortgage, owning three of the new white buildings in San Felice.

After exchanging pleasantries, the three leaders of the church remained on the open porch to greet the families as they reached the top of the trail, their freshly scrubbed children in tow. By seven o'clock the valley was dark, all the buggies had been hitched in circles to the walnut trees around the minister's cottage and the horses were neighing softly as they rubbed noses through the branches. Mrs Beaudry, president of the coffee club, came out of the kitchen ringing a cowbell. There was a good deal of friendly confusion as the men scrambled onto the long benches and their wives went to the serving table to heap plates with chicken and ham, goulash and enchiladas, salad, spaghetti, French bread and butter.

Having finished slicing the gingerbread, Margaret joined the three men on the porch. She nodded to the minister and August Hauser, then turned to her grandfather.

"Won't you come sit down, Gramp? I have a plate all filled for you."

"In a moment, Margaret. Mr Hauser's family hasn't arrived yet; I thought I'd wait with him."

The minister took a lingering look down the trail, then turned to Margaret.

"I guess I'd better go in and join the others," he murmured with a shading of regret, "so I'll accept your invitation, Miss Margaret."

"All right," she replied, "only I don't think you'll be able to handle Gramp's plate; it's pretty heavily loaded."

The three men chuckled, for Maxwell Widney's schoolboy appetite had already become a legend. As the clergyman walked inside with Margaret, John wondered what made the usually self-assured August agitatedly run his hand up and down the long gold watch chain he wore between his bottom vest pockets. August hauled out his heavy gold watch and studied it scowlingly, as though its face might reveal the reason why his wife and daughter were so late.

"They didn't get back from Los Angeles until five," he mumbled. "But even so, they said they were nearly ready when I left . . ."

Another quarter of an hour passed before they saw

False Witness

Mrs Hauser and Hilda mounting, a lantern between them. When they reached the porch, the girl considerably in advance, John noticed August's thick jaw drop with incredulity. Hilda was wearing, as understructure, one of the daring new corsets which gave an exaggerated curve to the hips in the back and sharply defined her bust; but what caused August's eyes to become as bloodshot red as his face was Hilda's resplendent new outfit, a baby-blue feather boa curled around a wide straw hat and a baby-blue silk gown edged with white lace, the sleeves full from elbow to wrist in the new bishop style, the shoulders considerably widened with epaulettes.

"Sorry to be late, Father," said Hilda, attempting to brush past. "It took so long to dress."

August reached out to catch his daughter by the arm.

"Where did you . . . ?"

He broke off and stood gaping. Hilda shook loose from his grasp, said, "Come, Mother," to the pale, frightened woman behind her and stepped through the door of the community house. All eyes turned toward her as she posed for an instant between August and John. From the quality of the gasp that went up, Hilda Hauser knew she had created the effect she desired.

Surveying the room swiftly to find Maxwell Widney, she full-sailed among the tables, confident the evening was hers.

As John watched her triumphal entry, he mused that no one in the history of Mission Valley had put such a strain on the Ninth Commandment; from the time she had matured at fifteen, Hilda's ripe red mouth, fluffy blonde hair and challenging green eyes had been a fount of potential gossip. The fact that the women of Mission Valley could not chatter did not mean they couldn't communicate. The older generation had developed a clairvoyance, the younger women a technique of uttering half sentences ending with a semicolon. When August Hauser had gone into Los Angeles, the November before, to choose an applicant for the position of minister, the women had merely commented, "August certainly picked a young and handsome clergyman"; there had been no need to add, "It will be a good match for his daughter." Now, as Maxwell Widney rose with shining face to make room for Hilda beside him, they turned to their friends and murmured, "What a beautiful dress August bought his daughter for the social"; their companions completed the sentence by thinking, "He's so stingy, only the prospect of landing the minister after all these months of trying could get him to loosen up."

After John had slipped onto the bench alongside Margaret and picked up a piece of Mrs Beaudry's fried chicken, he thought, "I'm glad for August's sake that Hilda fell in love with Widney. In fact, I'm glad for the community's sake."

When the hungry farmers had dispatched several plates of food, easing off with double portions of ice cream and cake, the young girls cleared the dishes while the boys arranged the benches for the entertainment. Mrs Celis' daughter played "Humoresque" on the fiddle; Mrs Wolkskill accompanied the oldest of her five sons in a group of *volklieder;* Henry Marden wheezed "O Sole Mio" on his accordion, and the young Atkinson boy made noises on his piccolo which caused him to take the instrument down from his mouth several times to look at it in hurt surprise.

Hilda Hauser and Maxwell Widney had waited for a discreet moment to slip out the door unnoticed. At nine o'clock, when the party was about to break up, Hilda reappeared with carmine spots high on her pretty cheeks. She went straight to August, whispering in his ear. August, who had been sitting with his paunch crushed against the plank table, not eating a bite nor hearing a note of the entertainment, expanded with the suddenness of a balloon into which hydrogen has been pumped. He rose, went to the table at the front of the room and rapped for order.

"Friends, I have news that I know you will all be happy to hear. I have the honor to announce the betrothal of my daughter Hilda to the Reverend Mr Maxwell Widney."

Everyone surged forward to surround Hilda and the blushing clergyman and offer his congratulations.

"When is the wedding to take place?" cried Mrs Beaudry.

"The first Sunday in June," replied Hilda with a charming flush. "I always wanted to be a June bride."

Later, as they walked down the trail to the clump of walnut trees, the women murmured to each other, "It 'll be a fine thing for Hilda"; out of years of precedent, out of years of reverence for John and the Annister plaque embedded in the front beam of their church, they refrained from adding, "Now she'll settle down."

3

JOHN WAS WORKING in his orange orchard the next morning when, through the clearing between the trees, he saw Margaret running toward him. He knew she had bicycled to the village not long before to do the marketing, for she had been manager of the household since she was fifteen. The jerky rhythm of her run told him at once that something was wrong. He dropped his plow handles and walked quickly to meet her.

"Gramp . . . there's trouble . . . in town."

"Trouble? What kind of trouble?"

"The Widow Smithers . . . she came running out of her cottage . . . screaming somebody stole her fifty dollars."

False Witness

John Annister's blue eyes deepened.

"The Widow Smithers . . . fifty dollars?"

"She claims she had it Tuesday, and this morning it's gone."

"Where would the Widow Smithers get fifty dollars?"

"Gramp, I haven't told you yet . . . She says Mary Shoe stole the money!"

His lean body recoiled as though he had been struck.

"Mary Shoe!"

"You remember when Mary left here Tuesday afternoon she said she was going to the widow's?"

"Yes."

"The widow claims her money disappeared while Mary was there."

"The Widow Smithers had no fifty dollars. If she did, no one stole it. If someone did, it wasn't Mary Shoe."

"There was a crowd gathered in front of her cottage when I left, Gramp."

"Then we'd better get there too."

"I sent word to have the mare hitched up."

The hired man was holding the mare's head, with the buggy pointed toward San Felice. John and Margaret jumped in from either side and drove east across the narrow wooden bridge, the boards clack-clacking under their wheels.

"I don't like this business," said John, looking straight ahead. "Even if it's only the widow's wild talk, it's dangerous. We never courted trouble in Mission Valley, and we never had none."

As he drove along the road between Philip Neill's silver-gray walnut trees and Joe Atkinson's foot-high corn, he mused that it was no accident this protected valley had lived so tranquilly. The clean hot sun had burned away meanness and greed; the interweaving of furrow patterns against the hills, the five receding ranges of the Sierra Madres, a solid mass of rose-lavender light at sunset, the fragrances of wild lilac, orange blossoms and jasmine had imbued the people with a touch of poetry and made the humblest as rich as his neighbor. A few of the children growing up had hungered for the outside world and had set forth to explore its mysteries; minor accidents had caused minor disputes, as when one man's hog had broken into another man's patch, or someone had taken too much irrigation water, leaving his neighbor too little; but for the better part the families had settled their differences on an amiable basis; their children had remained to work and save and buy land in the valley of their birth.

False Witness

It was only a ten-minute ride downhill until they reached San Felice, its one block of shops nestled in a tree-green oasis. Kearney's drugstore came first, with its round glass jars of red and green liquid, then Banning's general supply store, with leather harnesses setting in the window next to women's calico aprons and bonnets. On the left was Henry Marden's notion-and-stationery shop with the hand printing press at the back, while opposite was August Hauser's imposing brick building, one side of which he rented to the government for a post office. Hiram Hogarth's smithy was at the east end of the block, just across from the O'Melvany grocery store with its open straw-colored sacks of beans, rice, sugar and flour. The church board, which also acted as the town board in such matters as assessing taxes to build the wooden bridge across the river or pave the street in front of the block of stores against the driving winter rains, had decreed that all buildings in the village be painted white; and so they were.

At the end of the business block a number of homes lined the main valley road, shaded by pepper trees. The Widow Smithers' was the last of the group to the east, a tiny vine-covered cottage that had been left to the church by its owner and which the widow was permitted to occupy after her husband died. For the first time in the thirteen years since the widow had moved into the house, the people of the town were gathered in front of it.

John tied the mare to a hitching post on the opposite side of the road. When he pushed through the crowd they fell back, murmuring his name. At the topmost of the three threadbare steps was a crabbed woman of seventy-two with streaky white hair and a face of flesh pockets that broke in numerous bisecting planes. They stood staring at each other, the man who for thirty-five years had worked for unity among his neighbors, the old woman who stood on the threshold of shattering it.

"What's this all about, Widow Smithers?"

The old woman's watery eyes filled as she trembled before the sternness in his voice.

"They stole my fifty dollars!"

"Where did you get fifty dollars?"

"When Smithers died. I found five ten-dollar bills hid in his trunk. I kept them hid ever since."

"When did you see them last?"

"I counted them Tuesday morning. When I looked just now they was gone."

"Can you prove you had those greenbacks?"

False Witness

The widow peered at him uncertainly.

"Prove? I held them in my hands and counted them nearly every day since Smithers died."

"Did you show them? Did anyone know you had them?"

"I kept them hid, I tell you. They was all I had."

John made an impatient gesture.

"Who has been in the house since you saw the money last?"

"Only Mary Shoe."

"Surely you don't think Mary Shoe would take your money?"

"Yes, I do."

"But why? She couldn't have done a thing like that."

The widow's toothless jaw set.

"She took the money."

"Aren't you ashamed of yourself? Mary Shoe is the best friend you have in the world."

"She baked for me on Tuesday," cried the old woman shrilly. "She was in my flour barrel."

Puzzled, John looked at the faces nearest him in the crowd.

"That's where she claims she kept her money, John," said Ralph Banning, owner of the supply store.

John turned back to the widow.

"You kept your money in the flour barrel?"

"I hid it on the bottom, all folded up tight-like. Mary must have found it when she was taking out flour for my bread."

A gasp went up from the crowd. John silenced them with an angry look. His eyes sought his granddaughter's.

"Margaret, do you know where Mary is working?"

"Let's see, this is Thursday morning . . . She'll be at the Beaudrys'."

"Please bring her as fast as you can. But don't tell her what's wanted."

"Very well, Gramp."

When Margaret had driven off, John mounted the three steps to the widow's porch.

"Widow Smithers, for how many years has Mary Shoe been baking your bread?"

"Nigh onto ten, I reckon. Ever since I was took with the rheumatism."

"Has she been going into your flour barrel all these years?"

"Yes."

"If Mary has been in your flour barrel so many times, why didn't she ever find the money before?"

False Witness

"I don't know nothing about all that. All I know, my money's gone."

"Assuming she did find those bills yesterday, do you think Mary Shoe is the kind of woman who would steal your money? She's given you a hundred times fifty dollars' worth of work and never wanted a penny for it, not even when we offered it to her from the church fund."

"My money's gone," repeated the widow stolidly. "Mary was in my flour barrel, and my fifty dollars is gone."

From the manner in which some of the women were nodding their heads, John could see they had followed the widow's reasoning. He feared lest they confuse an accusation with a conviction.

"Keep questioning her, John," urged Hiram Hogarth, the village blacksmith.

John lit a match to his hastily stuffed pipe before looking at the widow again.

"Were you out of the house either Tuesday or Wednesday?"

"Yes, I went avisiting."

"Which day?"

"Both."

"Did you lock your door when you went out?"

"Now you know perfectly well, John Annister, nobody locks their door in San Felice."

"Then what would have prevented some vagrant from taking the money?"

"They could have got into the house all right, but there ain't a man living would think to look in the bottom of a flour barrel."

Several women said, "She's right. No man would have looked there."

This robbery was the most dramatic event to happen in Mission Valley in many a year. News of it spread rapidly. Those families whose farms were close by drove into town in their wagons, dressed as they had come out of the fields and kitchens. The road was lined on either side by horses and rigs of all sorts; the young folk pedaled in on their bicycles, which now littered the widow's lawn. By the time Margaret returned with Mary Shoemaker, there were almost a hundred people jammed in front of the widow's cottage, all talking at once. When they saw Margaret and Mary get out of the Annister buggy, they hushed.

"Mary," said John quietly, "when you left my house on Tuesday you said you were going to the Widow Smithers'."

"That's so, Mr John."

False Witness

"Did you go into her flour barrel that afternoon?"

"You can't bake bread without you use flour."

"Mary, did you see any ten-dollar bills on the bottom of that barrel?"

Mary gazed at him as though he had lost possession of his senses, then popped out with the thought that had come first into everyone's mind.

"What would the Widow Smithers be doing with ten-dollar bills?"

"That doesn't answer my question, Mary."

"No. I never saw no bills."

"The widow says she kept five of them hidden on the bottom of her flour barrel. She says she saw them there Tuesday morning, and this morning they're gone."

Mary stood with her head cast down, thinking out the implications of what John had said. When she raised her eyes to look at the widow, he saw in them neither anger nor bitterness, but deep hurt.

"Mr John, you don't think I took that money?"

"Did you, Mary?" he asked gently.

Mary shrunk from the ring of faces that seemed to be pressing closer upon her. She took a sighing breath before answering.

"No, Mr John, I didn't see no money and I didn't take none."

"I knew you hadn't, Mary; I didn't ask that question for myself. I wanted you to tell it to these people here, so the matter could be closed."

"That don't get me back my fifty dollars," screamed the widow. "It was all I had in the world. It kept me from being a pauper."

"I'm not saying you never had the fifty dollars," replied John in tones of finality. "I'm saying that if you did have it, you never needed it. The church has supported you all these years and is perfectly able to take care of you for the rest of your life. For your own sake, as well as ours, forget about those bills on the bottom of your flour barrel. When trouble is made among people who aren't used to trouble, it can cause a heap of damage."

"That's so, John," affirmed Ralph Banning and Kearney, the druggist.

"Looks like a lot of us will be eating cold dinners if we don't get home right smart," said John, waving his hand to the crowd. "Come, Mary, Margaret and I will give you a lift back to your work."

4

AUGUST HAUSER came to call on the Annisters that
evening. Grace, who never got over being frightened
at August's loud voice, ran to her bedroom when she
heard him booming at the front door. Margaret pulled
up a chair for him to the round oak table that stood
on four hand-carved animal paws. The light from the
kerosene lamp with its green glass shade illumined their
faces but left the rest of the room in darkness. August
pushed aside the copy of *The Conquest of Canaan* that
Margaret had been reading; he did not approve of
novels for young people. It was evident to John there
was something on August's mind.

"Bad business, the Widow Smithers' fifty dollars,"
commented August.

"Mighty bad."

"I hear that you . . . eh . . . conducted an investigation."

"Not exactly. I just wanted to spike . . ."

"That's the function of the justice of the peace," interrupted August. "That's why the people of the valley elect me to office."

"I'm sorry, August, I didn't mean . . . But when Mary Shoe was falsely accused . . ."

"Are you so sure she was falsely accused?"

"As positive as that you're sitting across my table."

"After all, John, she's a poor woman. She has a hard time keeping up that acre farm of hers."

"Being poor and being a thief aren't the same."

August did not hear the interruption; when he was discussing an important matter he listened only to his own thoughts.

"Just imagine what a temptation it would be for a woman in her position to find five ten-dollar greenbacks. She might have taken them without intending to steal them. She might even think that someone else put them there and they didn't belong to the widow at all."

"August, you remember ten years ago when Margaret came down with the typhoid? Mary Shoe sat up with her for three days and nights without hardly a wink of sleep. Doctor said he mightn't have pulled her through without Mary. When I tried to pay her for her time, she wouldn't take more 'n her regular two dollars a day. A woman like that don't steal."

"Things happen to people, John. They develop needs. Temptation is sometimes too much for them."

"Yes, August, that's true, but not with people who have character. Circumstances change, but good character is enduring."

August massaged his heavy watch chain for a pondering moment, then smiled. He had a good smile when he permitted himself to use it.

"As a matter of fact, John, I agree with you. I don't believe Mary Shoe took that money. I'm not even sure it existed."

"Then that's the end of the matter?"

"Unless someone was to file a complaint. But nobody's going to do that. I don't think there 'll be much talk in the valley either; but just to make sure, I'll have my future son-in-law preach a sermon on the Ninth Commandment next Sunday."

{ 5 {

THE FIRST THING John noted out of the ordinary the next afternoon was the strained position of the three men leaning over the counter of Banning's. When they turned to say, "Howdy, John," their faces were flushed, as though they had snapped a conversation hame. One by one they took their packages and walked out.

"They were talking about the Widow Smithers' fifty dollars," said John a little sadly.

Ralph Banning, who usually was as straightforward as the weather bulletins he kept posted over his cash till, avoided his friend's gaze.

"John, haven't you . . . heard?" he asked almost unwillingly.

False Witness

"Heard what?"

"About Hilda Hauser?"

"I haven't heard anything."

"She was seen coming out of the Widow Smithers' house Tuesday morning. The widow was visiting and didn't even know she had been there."

Uneasy, baffled, John asked, "What was Hilda doing in the widow's house?"

"Oh, she goes to gab with the old lady sometimes when she's in town and has nothing better to do."

John turned his head slowly from left to right to follow the curving arc of his thoughts.

"Who saw her?"

"Albert Ross."

"I'd best go talk to Ross. If you see anyone driving out my road, will you ask them to tell Margaret I'll be late for supper?"

"I'll do that little thing, John."

Riding behind his mare along the north road, John mused that the mills of the gods grind exceeding small. Though there had been differences between him and August, only once had they come to words: over Albert Ross. August had foreclosed a mortgage against Ross and moved him off his farm. When John had accused him of loving his dollars better than his neighbors, August had replied:

45

False Witness

"Dollars are the tools of my trade. If I took less care of them than you do of your plows, would you think better of me?"

John had been able to voice no adequate reply. Time, he decided, had now given an answer.

Where the valley floor began to rise sharply into the Sierra Madres, John turned into the acres Ross had rented when August dispossessed him. Ross was a juiceless fellow who had been farming all his life without discovering he had no talent for the job; already the yard was littered with fragments of broken machinery. When John whoaed his mare, August broke off the argument he was having with Ross and walked with agitated steps to the Annister buggy.

For five long years August Hauser had been enduring the harrowing anxiety of the father who realizes that at any moment, while he is working at his desk or sleeping in his bed, word can be brought that his flighty daughter has disgraced the family. No one knew better than August that any scandal breaking over Hilda's head would necessarily involve her father, that he would have to resign as justice of the peace and president of the church board, that his prestige and very life would be shattered. Every bite August ate, every word that passed his lips, was flavored with gnawing fear. From the despair on his face as he looked up pleadingly at John it was clear that the most prominent citizen of Mission Valley was afraid the long-dreaded catastrophe had caught up with him.

"John, you've got to help me."

Watching August run the back of a hand roughly across his bloodshot eyes, John realized that never before had he seen the arrogant Hauser with his defenses down.

"I don't know why this should happen to me," said August in a hoarse voice. "I've always been a God-fearing man. I've lived up to the law and done my duty. All my life I've worked for the best interests of our church and our community. I've never done harm; I've never cheated anyone . . ."

John remained silent, observing how haggard August's sagging neck muscles made him look. August misread his friend's silence for lack of sympathy with his plight. Then he recalled the words he had had with John over the dispossessing of Albert Ross.

"You're thinking I made people pay me interest on the money I loaned them," he continued, his wind coming hard, "and if they couldn't pay I took their property. But think of all those whose property I saved because I had the funds to lend them when they were up against it. Money has a right to earn interest, John. My dollars worked in the valley fields same as men did, and they earned their wage same as men did. That's plain business."

John answered in his gentle drawl, but there was no twinkle in the blue eyes he kept fastened on August.

"Yes, you always lived according to what you thought was right. But what you thought was right and what I thought was right wasn't always the same. My dollars sometimes plowed another man's furrows too, but I didn't expect them to earn me any wages. That's what extra money is for, to help your neighbor when he's hard put, so he can help you when you're hard put."

August stared out across the valley toward the Santa Monica hills, unseeing.

"I always been a proud man, John; no one knows that better 'n you. When I looked out the window of my office today . . . I could see people talking about me . . . some of them triumphant . . . some with pity in their eyes . . ."

John slid his long legs out of the buggy.

"Easy does it, August."

"I told you last night I didn't believe the Widow Smithers had any fifty dollars," said August quickly.

"Even if she had, what would Hilda be doing in her flour barrel? Hilda may have given me some cause for worry, but she isn't dishonest . . . she wouldn't take the widow's money."

"I know that, August."

"Then see what you can do to quiet Ross. He hates me; he's glad for the chance to talk about Hilda."

"What hurts you hurts Mission Valley. I'll do all I can to keep trouble in its own pasture."

Together the two men walked up the path to where Ross was fumbling with the makings of a cigarette.

"Albert, why did you do this?" asked John.

"You think I'm lying too?" cried Ross, spilling the tobacco from the brown paper. "You don't believe I seen Hilda come out the widow's house? She was wearing that pink dress with the sash and the pink hair ribbon . . ."

John raised his hand to stop the rush of words.

"You're going to cause us a heap of trouble, friend."

"I ain't told nobody but the Lowdens across the road," said Ross, sotto voce. "Besides, I don't see it's going to cause you no trouble; it ain't your daughter."

John's close-trimmed white mustache bristled; he was not so gentle of nature he wouldn't fight for the things he loved.

False Witness

"You been in Mission Valley six years now and you still don't know what we stand for, that what hurts one of us hurts us all. Looks like I should have let you leave the valley, instead of getting this farm for you."

Ross's faded eyes filled with tears.

"I'm sorry, John. I didn't mean no wrong. I heared they was accusing Mary Shoe, and since I seen Hilda coming out the house the day the money was took . . ." His eyes went from John's face to August's, then down to the ground. "I'll go tell 'em I'm a skunken liar if you think it 'll help."

"That's exactly what you're going to do," cried August.

John restrained August's threatening gesture, then indicated the house across the road.

"Too late for that now, August. Mrs Lowden and her daughter-in-law are watching us from the porch. If someone should think we put Ross up to saying he lied, they'd wonder what we were trying to hide."

August swung his hand back and forth on the gold watch chain; then, as though gathering strength from the gesture, slowly straightened up and squared his shoulders.

"This is going to make things mighty bad for Mary Shoe," he said in his usual dictatorial tone.

False Witness

John blinked at the sudden change in August's manner.

"For Mary Shoe?"

"Last night," broke in August, "every family in the valley talked about Mary Shoe and the Widow Smithers' fifty dollars, but by this morning there wasn't anything new left to say. Tonight every family is talking about my Hilda and the fifty dollars, and the case is open again. If the people of Mission Valley have to choose between my daughter and Mary Shoe . . ."

When he reached home, John found Grace seated at the dining-room table, her usually dull, flaccid face gleaming with excitement. She had run a wet comb through her hair and donned her black taffeta dress. She waited for Margaret to serve her grandfather before speaking.

"So our high and mighty Hilda has taken a tumble!" she exclaimed. "She was too good for this valley . . . she wasn't going to be a hick . . . she was going to a big city and live like a lady. Well, we might be hick farmers, but we're not so low we'd steal a poor widow's money."

"You have no right to accuse Hilda."

"She was seen coming out of the house, wasn't she?"

"Yes, but she often visits the . . ."

"Then she picked the wrong day this time."

John had always known how bitterly Grace resented what she called Hilda's loose ways with the boys. If the other women of the valley, most of whom Hilda had offended with her superior attitudes, harbored equally burning resentments, then he knew she was in for a rough time.

"Oh, come, Grace," he coaxed, "August pulled the reins on her pretty tight, and she kicked over the traces, that's all. She never did anything really bad."

"She did this time. We all knew she would."

Margaret had been sitting with her eyes fastened on her plate, the color mounting slowly in her cheeks. She threw up her head with an angry look.

"Mother, it's downright mean of you to say such things."

The light faded from Grace's face. She pushed aside her untouched food and rose.

"Hilda won't get the minister now," she exulted as she escaped toward her bedroom. "He wouldn't dare marry a thief!"

6

AT SUNDOWN EVERY SATURDAY the population of Mission Valley collected in San Felice to buy its supplies, chat with its neighbors, smoke a friendly pipe or share a bag of peanut brittle. John had always enjoyed these hours at the end of the week's work, but this evening, as he and Margaret rode into town, he had misgivings.

"It feels like a summer storm rising in New Hampshire," he murmured as San Felice appeared through the ash-gray haze that had hung over the valley all day. "Clouds begin to gather, suddenly the air is still, there doesn't seem to be enough of it to breathe, and a heaviness sits on your spirit."

He shook his head sadly. San Felice looked like a

strange village, one he had never seen before. There was no hearty laughter, no movement of neighbors from group to group, no backslapping, handshaking, storytelling. People stood in tight circles in front of the stores where they had shopped, talking in undertones, each group watching the other from the corner of its eye. Instead of the warm greetings that had always welcomed him, faces were averted in guilt.

"Gramp, we ought not be here," said Margaret, as the mare turned into her usual hitching post in front of Marden's notion store. "I can do my shopping some other time."

John looked at her with a start: for the moment he had imagined himself back in New Hampshire, hearing his mother issue one of her soft-spoken commands designed to save the menfolk of her family from unnecessary hurt.

"I think you're right, Margaret."

He backed the buggy around and once again drove through the block of stores. Every face turned to watch him go. If he had deliberately struck his friends, he could not have censured them more forcibly.

When they reached home they found Norman Martell waiting for them under the oak. Norman was a sweet-mannered chap of twenty-four with a shock of curly brown hair, warm brown eyes and a smiling sun-burned face. He had begun swimming at the Annister dam shortly after Margaret had been born. First, because Norman took such solicitous care of little Margaret, later, because of his gentle straightforward disposition, John had come to think of the boy as a son, giving to him all the confidence and affection he would have lavished on the son he had lost when he lost his Margarita.

Norman held up his arms to help Margaret out of the buggy, their lips touching in a welcoming kiss for the brief instant before her feet touched the ground.

"We thought you weren't coming, Norman," said John, clasping the boy's outstretched hand. "It got so late."

"I had some work to prepare for Monday morning."

"That's right, son; work comes first. How you getting on with the law?"

Norman had been practicing law in Los Angeles for only a year, since his graduation the previous spring.

"Well, I won two small cases last week."

"You won two cases in court?" cried Margaret proudly.

"I kept us out of court," the young man answered. "The place to win cases is in your office."

John nodded approvingly to Margaret.

"Didn't I say he'd make a good lawyer?"

Margaret looked up at Norman with the fragment of a smile he had learned to cherish when she was a child of six and John Annister had entrusted her to his care each morning to see her safely to school.

"Yes, Gramp, you always said so."

Because Norman had a small body and was soft-spoken, because he lacked aggressiveness and a gift of the gab, he had met with opposition when he announced he was going to leave his father's prosperous asparagus ranch to enter the law college in Los Angeles. Only John, who had watched the boy devour the books in Margarita's sitting room, knew him to have a capacity for cool logical thinking.

After their supper of rare roast beef, Boston baked beans and brown bread, a heritage from John's youth in New England, Grace delighted them by offering to do the dishes alone. When John went into Margarita's little sitting room to smoke his pipe, the young couple strolled out of doors. The shrubbery that covered the lower part of the house was fast coming into bloom, the white button flowers already appearing on the tobirus, the oleander bushes a mass of tight red buds. Margaret's hand lightly in his, they walked from shrub to shrub, examining the jets of fresh spring foliage.

Norman had once called Margaret a Latin Yankee, a name which delighted her because she was entirely conscious of the two blood streams housed harmoniously under her skin. As she turned to him her sensitive, pastel-complected face, framed in its background of rich black hair, he was glad he had been told about Margarita, for that helped him to understand Margaret. He knew that from John she had inherited her gentle nature, her shrewd observation and dry sense of humor, from Margarita, her fierce loyalty.

"Norm, you know about the Widow Smithers' money?"

"My dad told me."

"It seems such a little thing, only fifty dollars, but if you could have felt the . . . the tension in town this afternoon . . ." She shuddered. "You know how Gramp feels when something goes wrong in the valley: as though his own child was sick in bed. Do what you can to reassure him, will you?"

They joined John in Margarita's little sitting room, with its red damask drapes, silver candelabrum and shelves of old leather-bound books. This room was sacred to John; Norman was the only one outside the family allowed to enter it. A number of years before,

False Witness

John had yielded to the eager look on the boy's face whenever he stood by Margarita's piano, touching the yellow keys, and had suggested that Norman take lessons on it from Mrs Marden's spinster sister. Now, as he sat on his low-lying tapestry-covered rocker, listening to Norman play and Margaret sing the same Spanish ballads Margarita had sung to him, he thought how endless time was and how enduring its patterns.

"Norman, I suppose you've heard about the trouble we're having?"

"Yes sir."

"Hilda has aroused antagonism in this valley; it's likely to work against her. On the other hand, August Hauser has a lot of families in his debt . . ."

Norman wound his right index finger through his curly brown hair.

"From what I hear, there's serious doubt as to whether the widow had the fifty dollars. I don't think you need be anxious about Mary; nobody can think her guilty. And if there's some suspicion of Hilda, after all, she's August's concern, not yours. I'd be inclined to call it a tempest in a teapot."

"It isn't the guilt of Mary. It isn't the guilt of Hilda. It isn't even the disappearance of the fifty dollars. What you call a tempest in a teapot might become a great storm and engulf the people of this valley, who up to the present have lived together in brotherly love."

"Then we'll make every effort to see that the storm doesn't come up," said Norman, taking on John's seriousness. "I'll stay in the valley next week if you think I can be of any help."

John rose, knocked out his pipe against the side of the ash tray.

"No, no, son; you go back to your office. We've always worked things out here friendly like. I'm sure we can this time. . . . Well, I know you youngsters have a lot to tell each other, so I'll trundle off to bed. You'll go to church with us tomorrow, won't you?"

Norman walked to the door of John's bedroom and bade him good night. When he returned to Margaret he was unsmiling. He sat on the low piano bench beside her and began improvising, as he often did when he had a problem to think out.

"Margaret, I'm afraid Gramp is right: the valley may be in for trouble."

"But if they can't prove anything? Sooner or later they'll wear out their interest."

"That's just it: they can prove something."

"Against whom?"

False Witness

"Let's state the facts: Hilda was seen coming out of the widow's house on Tuesday. Early Wednesday morning she and her mother go to Los Angeles. Wednesday evening Hilda comes to the social in a beautiful new gown, the most expensive she has ever owned. Everyone knows how stingy August has been with his family. Doesn't it strike you as something more than a coincidence that Hilda should buy the most expensive gown of her life on the day after the widow's money disappeared?"

The candle ends sputtered in their hot wax base. Margaret made no move to replace them.

"Mightn't August spend that much . . . as an investment?" she asked tentatively. "Hilda has been so unhappy in Mission Valley; she's wanted to move away so badly. Marrying her to the minister was his one chance of quieting her and keeping her here."

"I hope you're right, Margaret, but I doubt it. From the way I hear August behaved at the social the other night, he was more stunned by Hilda's new dress than anyone else. Somebody is sure to put two and two together."

Margaret sat quietly for a moment, her hands folded in her lap.

"That's going to make it hard on Hilda," she said.

"Not so hard as on Mary—and your Gramp."

He felt her slender figure stiffen. In the pause before she spoke, he observed how she changed in times of stress, her blue eyes widening and becoming black, her color deepening to match her feelings until she was a replica of the picture of Margarita Abila which hung over John's bed.

"Why do you say that, Norman?" she asked in a low tone.

"Because the closer Mission Valley comes to making a case against Hilda, the surer you can be that August will try to fasten the guilt on Mary Shoe."

} 7 {

WHEN JOHN AND MARGARET rose at six the next morning, they found Grace already in the kitchen, heating a tub of water on the wood stove for her bath.

"What are you doing up so early?" asked John. "You always sleep till noon on Sundays."

"I'm going to church."

"Church! Except to look at the new minister, you haven't been in church for two years."

Grace pushed up the sleeves of her flannel bathrobe, lifted the tub off the stove by its two iron handles and made for the bathroom.

"But I'm going this morning. Everybody'll be there."

False Witness

When the bathroom door had closed behind his daughter, John said, "This is the first time in her life I've seen your mother excited about going to church."

Norman arrived at eight, walking up the riverbank from the south, where the Annister and Martell farms shared a common border. His curly brown hair was still wet from the bath, and he was wearing a polka-dot necktie that made him seem younger than his twenty-four years. Margaret was waiting for him on the front porch. She watched his soft brown eyes open wide and beam with pride as he saw her standing slim and straight in her new percale suit.

Grace insisted they take the buggy for the quarter-mile journey to the clump of wild walnuts. When they had tethered the mare and gone halfway up the trail, Margaret turned to her grandfather.

"Gramp, would you hold the prayer books? Norman and I'll gather some flowers for Grandma's grave."

John watched the young couple climb onto the side of the hill, thick with blue lupin. Below him the Santa Monica mountains rolled downward with soft and sensuous curves; opposite, the Sierra Madres were hard, promontory. Between lay the fertile crotch of earth, taking its seed, giving forth its fruit.

False Witness

When Margaret and Norman returned with arms full of flowers, they continued upward past the church to the cemetery on the crest, where the trail crossed from Santa Monica. To the west, they could see the blue waters of the Pacific resting quietly in a lagoon; to the east, the valley sky was a brittle turquoise after the storm. Every tree, every blade of grass, stood out in stark clarity. Fugitive clouds lay elongated rain shadows across vivid green fields, and the bare peach and walnut groves stood out like forests of purple sticks. Through the rain-washed air the distant Sierra Madres seemed as close as the rail fence around a man's farm, yet the valley appeared wider and more richly cultivated than ever. This was the very ground where young John Annister had first tramped over the mountains from Santa Monica; this was the place where he and Margarita had often come of an evening when the moon filled their valley with a luminous white mist.

"Margarita always said we ought to be buried here when our time came," John murmured while Margaret covered the grave with lupin, "because then the valley would be ours forever. When she died and I brought her up here, it was just a lonely grave on the side of a hill. It brought me comfort to know that she was resting in the most beautiful spot on God's earth, and that one day I would rest here beside her."

Margaret turned to look at her grandfather's face. She found no sadness, only the serenity of a man who has already lived forever. She wanted to reproach him for thinking of death when he was so young and strong, but she knew that for John Annister death was a friend who would reunite him with the woman he loved. Her mind went back to the day she had first stood by this grave, and her grandfather had told her stories of her lovely grandmother; then, as now, his lean weather-parched face had glowed when he spoke of the magnificent view from this knoll above his small world.

They retraced their path down from the knoll to the church, mounting the front steps. As John stood looking up at the Annister plaque he took from his vest pocket the steel-rimmed spectacles he wore when reading the Bible or attending services. He had no need for the glasses—he never used them for any other kind of reading—but he felt one should not go naked to the Word. John, Grace and Margaret entered the church and slipped into the Annister pew, the third from the front on the left. Norman joined his family just behind them. Across and one pew forward, sat

False Witness

August Hauser; on one side of him, his wife, her head bowed, on the other, Hilda, scanning brightly the expressions of her neighbors as they entered. The church filled quickly with its freshly scrubbed congregation, for Mission Valley believed that cleanliness came next to godliness in time as well as spirit. The Timothy Temples greeted the Annisters with their usual smile as they slipped into the pew in front; the Wolkskills nodded as they took their seats opposite; but the Beaudrys kept their faces stonily forward as they passed the Annisters, smiling only to the Hausers. There was a feeling of stifled excitement that clashed with the tranquillity of the church and made John Annister sore of heart.

He was relieved when the Reverend Mr Maxwell Widney, in his freshly pressed black suit and shining white collar, entered from the rear of the pulpit. He looked strong and calm. The fugitive feeling of antagonism faded as the congregation lifted its face to this honest and sincere young preacher.

"Jonathan Waite found he was not the only minister of God in this valley. He found what should be true in every Christian community: that you were all ministers of God, bringing kindness and sympathy to your neighbors, lending succor when succor was needed

keeping alive the faith and love that binds humans together. Into the front beam of your church you built
the Ninth Commandment. Into your hearts you built
the proverb: 'Behold how beautiful it is for brothers
to dwell together in harmony.' If you begin by teach-
ing your neighbor to distrust his neighbor, he will
end by distrusting you. If you violate your Ninth
Commandment, if you pluck that most profoundly
true of all proverbs out of your hearts, you will destroy yourselves."

From the cleared atmosphere of the church, John
thought the minister had led them safely out of the
wilderness; but his confidence lasted only until the
following Tuesday morning, when Mary Shoemaker
came to work with puffed eyes and fatigue lines sunk
between her cheeks and nose.

"You still worrying, Mary?" he asked. "It will all
be forgotten by the end of the week. There isn't a
soul in Mission Valley thinks you took the money."

"Yes, there is, Mr John."

"Who?"

"The Beaudrys. When I come to work yesterday
afternoon she said she's sorry, she can't use me no
more."

Mary began crying silently; two big tears slipped

slowly over the crest of her cheeks. Death she had been able to understand, aloneness, hard labor all the years of her life; but this charge of robbing a neighbor appeared to leave her stunned and helpless. John, too, was stunned. For a long time no word was spoken in the Annister kitchen.

"I was going to spray my trees this morning," said John at length, "but it looks like the aphis can eat into other things besides fruit."

It was no short walk to the Beaudrys': down the river past the Martells', east along the irrigation ditches past the Wolkskill and Temple farms, then diagonally across the Neill walnut orchards; but John covered the ground quickly with his long perturbed strides. He found Beaudry in his barn doing his early morning chores. Beaudry was a bald-headed man of thirty-seven with dry cracked lips and a deeply clefted chin from which he rarely succeeded in shaving all the black beard.

"Morning, John," he called, glancing up for a second from the milking stool. "Nice morning."

"Don't feel nice to me, Bill," replied John. "Feels like kinda mean morning to me."

"Why, what's eating on you?"

False Witness

"You."

"Me?"

"Bill, you know that Mary Shoe never took the money. If you pretend you think she did, for no matter what reason, if you make that poor woman look guilty before the whole valley, you're doing something more dishonest than whoever stole the fifty dollars."

Beaudry straightened up from his crouch and kicked the milking stool out from under him. Frightened, the cow swerved around, upsetting the pail.

"Whoa, not so fast, John; you're running away with the wagon. The missus and I are sure Mary took the money when she found it in the flour barrel."

"Mary's helped out in your house for fifteen years; did you ever miss so much as a pin?"

Beaudry ran his thumb down through the deep crevice in his chin.

"It's our opinion Mary took the money, and it's our opinion we're entitled to our opinion."

John crinkled his perplexity around his innocent eyes.

"Bill Beaudry, I've known you ever since I sat out here in this very barn with your daddy, waiting for you to be borned. In all these years I don't recollect you told me a lie."

"Don't recollect I did."

"That makes it too late to start now, don't it?" the older man asked pleadingly.

Beaudry's face and fists clenched. Then he remembered it was John Annister, loosened his anger, set the stool upright and resumed his milking.

"Anytime 'd be too late," he replied without looking up.

John left the Beaudry farm with his eyes on the earth, walking slowly. A truth-telling man himself, it was difficult for him to believe Beaudry capable of an outright lie; yet it was even more difficult for him to believe that anyone could honestly think Mary Shoemaker guilty.

He heard mingled deep and high laughter come out of the green alfalfa fields ahead, where Herman Wolkskill was working with his five sons. John left the irrigation ditch and went into the Wolkskill field. Herman Wolkskill had come from Hungary as a boy of twelve, but he still retained his mid-European accent and his mid-European manners. He was the jolliest man in the valley; short, plump, with luxuriant mustaches that swept upward, a lover of laughter for its

70

own sake, with an omnivorous appetite for life, Herman had begat for Mission Valley thirteen children, a quartet to play Mozart, a choir for the church and an unending fund of hilarious anecdotes.

Herman and his five boys, all as plump and cheerful as himself, gave John a boisterous welcome.

"What takes you out to visiting so early, John?" Herman asked.

"I been over to see Bill Beaudry. He and his missus let Mary Shoe go yesterday."

"Because she stolen the widow's fifty dollars?"

"That's what they say."

Herman stopped filling his pipe, dumped the tobacco back into its can with a disgusted gesture and stuck them both into his overall pocket.

"So sure's my name's Herman Wolkskill, she don't take it, and Bill Beaudry know she don't take it."

"Beaudry's a good chap, he wouldn't . . ."

Herman flashed a family look to his five boys which read, "Close your ears, you don't hear this." Then he turned back to John with no trace of his perennial grin.

"Beaudry and August Hauser make money together on mortgages."

John stared straight in front of him.

False Witness

"I tried to keep that out of my mind. It don't seem reason enough. Herman, we got to fight this thing like we did the grasshopper plague four years ago."

"You count on me, John. Tell Mary Shoe she comes now to help on Monday afternoons the Wolkskills."

8

Up to the moment Bill Beaudry discharged Mary Shoemaker there had been little taking of sides in Mission Valley. Those who had long been scandalized by Hilda believed she took the widow's five green bills, those who believed the temptation had been too great thought Mary took them, but few said so outside the walls of their own homes. From two generations of tradition all public discussion of the theft confined itself to the bare statement of facts: the widow had kept five ten-dollar bills in her flour barrel; Mary Shoemaker was in the flour barrel the day they disappeared; Hilda Hauser was seen coming out of the widow's house that same day.

With Beaudry throwing down the gauge, the talk

became more open. Still cautiously veering away from the comparative guilt of Mary or Hilda, the valley discussed instead the merits of what Beaudry and Wolkskill had done. Those families that had always smothered their antagonism toward the Hausers said it was downright mean for Beaudry to fire Mary without the crime being proved against her, blessing Herman Wolkskill for his kindness. Those who felt an allegiance to August maintained that Beaudry had a right to hire and fire whomever he pleased, that Herman Wolkskill was a busybody who had better be careful about throwing dirt in Bill Beaudry's face. Neighborly discussions were beginning to be disced like adobe after the winter rains.

Late Wednesday afternoon John and Margaret were feeding the chickens when they saw Timothy Temple coming toward them, a shotgun under his arm. Tim was the valley's gamecock, a redheaded fellow who burned with the intensity of a blowtorch. When he had first come to the valley, the old settlers had looked askance at his five feet of height and hundred pounds of weight, telling each other that he couldn't possibly farm twenty acres. It had taken them but a short time to learn that Timothy was a stick of dynamite with a red cap, so tireless a worker that he would come in after twelve hours in the burning fields and, for relaxation, cultivate his rose garden. When he was out of earshot—for they had a vast respect for his flaming temper—they called him Tiny Tim. He and John had become devoted friends; each winter they packed into the Sierra Nevadas for a couple of weeks to hunt.

"The hills are covered with quail, John," said Timothy in his high voice. "What do you say we get ourselves a bag?"

John was puzzled; it was not like Tim to knock off before sundown. Besides, there was an unusual glint in his intense green eyes.

"All right, Tim. I'll get my gun."

"Can I come, Gramp? I haven't had any shooting since the rains started."

"Sure. Slip into your high boots; the spring sage will have the trails covered."

They crossed westerly to the Santa Monica mountains and, about a mile beyond the church, took a trail that wound through clumps of scrub oak and red-trunked sumac. After a stiff climb they came to a clearing; ahead was the canyon pass through which the quail and doves flew each evening from the valley to the sea. They lay prone in the high yellow mustard until the birds came winging, first in pairs, then in coveys. They let Margaret shoot first, then Tim, then John. When the passage was over, they climbed among the rocks to fill their brown canvas pouches. Tim squatted on a flat boulder with his gun held forward, surveying Mission Valley.

"John, I took Stella to the doctor in Los Angeles yesterday. On the way I got an idea. I asked her where Hilda would buy a dress like she wore to the social. Stella said most likely at the Bon Marché. So I went to the Bon Marché and asked the manager if he remembered the dress."

"Why did you do all that, Tim?"

"After he said he remembered fine, I said, 'Do you remember how it was paid for?'"

"Did he?" popped out Margaret.

"Certainly did. It was paid for with . . . ten-dollar greenbacks."

"But it still doesn't prove anything against Hilda," cried Margaret. "It's what Norman calls 'circumstantial evidence.' Any woman going shopping for a spring outfit might have carried money just that way."

"She might have," agreed Tim, "but it's an unlucky coincidence for Hilda."

After a pause John said softly, "Tim, it's not one of the things I like to know."

"It's one of the things you need to know."

"Why?"

"Remember when I bucked August on that land deal a few years ago? He whupped me . . . by tricks you and me wouldn't call fair."

"Yes, Tim, I remember. But I wouldn't want there to be a whupping in this—for anybody."

"Well," snapped Tim, "I just wanted to make sure it wasn't you and Mary got it in the neck."

John couldn't resist a tiny smile of gratitude.

"Wouldn't do any good for people to find out about this Bon Marché business, would it?"

"Nobody knows but Stella and my daughter."

By noon of the following day new fuel had been added to the gossip fires: everyone knew how Hilda had paid for her baby-blue dress. "Have you heard, Hilda gave the Bon Marché five ten-dollar bills for that dress." "Funny, ain't it, Hilda just happening to have those five greenbacks in her purse?" Tim Temple's long red hair stood up almost straight on his head as he came stalking through the Annister orange orchard.

"Doggone, John, Stella and my daughter swear they never said a word outside the house. The walls must have ears!"

"They always have. Tim, we're bogging down deeper all the time. Where will all this end? How will we put a stop to the gossiping now?"

There was an excited gleam in Tim's eye as he answered:

"Looks like it ain't going to stop till it's settled."

The people of Mission Valley had come to the same conclusion. Though they feared August too greatly to make open accusations, several of the farmers said over the front counter of Banning's store, "Ain't it about time August come to his daughter's defense?" Groups were now asking, "Did August know his daughter was coming to the social in a new dress? Did he give Hilda the money for it? Did he give it to her in ten-dollar bills?"

All afternoon people walked and drove past Hauser's whitewashed brick building, gazing at August as though he had changed in a few hours. August sat in his swivel chair before the roll-top desk in the big front window where he carried on his business of buying and selling produce, nodding as acquaintances passed. The passers-by revealed little of what they were thinking; August disclosed little of the turmoil going on beneath his heavy vest.

From long experience with August, the valley knew

that he would strike, but when the move came it was altogether unexpected. Maxwell Widney summoned the members of the church board for a special meeting for the following night.

"It was August called the board meeting," said Margaret that evening, as they sat under the patio oak in the cool, fragrant air.

"For twenty-five years we've been settling valley problems at the board meetings," said John, puffing slowly on his pipe. "That's the place to settle this one too."

"Yes, I guess so," she replied, "but I don't like it. Because you're defending Mary Shoe, August thinks he's fighting you. Remember what Tim said yesterday: August doesn't fight fair. . . . Gramp, can I drive the mare to Glendale tomorrow afternoon? Norman was coming out on Saturday anyway; I'm sure he'd come tomorrow instead, if he thought we needed him. I can market and exchange my books at the library while waiting for his train."

"Why disturb Norman? He has work to do."

"He can bring his books home with him. I'd like to have him here."

"I'd rather you wouldn't, Margaret."

"But you don't forbid it?"

"No, I don't forbid it."

She was waiting at the little redwood station in Glendale at five-forty the next afternoon when Norman alighted from the train with a bulging portmanteau under his arm. While they shook hands shyly, Margaret thought with pride and tenderness how businesslike he looked in his heavy suit.

"Did I take you away from anything important, Norman?" she asked as they walked the few steps to the buggy.

"There's nothing in Los Angeles as important to me as . . . well . . . Mission Valley. You know that, Margaret."

"Yes, my dear," she murmured, her slender young face turned up to his.

When they began driving into the setting sun, Norman said, "Now tell me everything that's happened. Start at the beginning and don't leave out a detail."

Margaret told the full story. Norman listened attentively, asking an occasional question. When they reached Mission Oaks, they found Mary Shoemaker waiting to serve dinner, so no word was mentioned about the fifty dollars until she had washed the dishes and left for home.

"Would there be any chance of your taking me to

that board meeting tonight, Gramp?" asked Norman.

"Why, no, son. The meetings are for members only." He laid a hand affectionately on the young man's shoulder. "I've battled my way through hundreds of board meetings and it never done me no harm. I can take care of myself."

At the rear door to the church John paused to take his spectacles from their case and don them. Thus fortified, he entered the board room with its unpainted plank walls and two plain windows up near the ceiling. Maxwell Widney was sitting at the head of the hand-carved black mahogany table Symon Maller had brought around Cape Horn in a sailing vessel and willed to the church. August Hauser was at his right, Ralph Banning, smelling faintly of the fresh leather and oil of his store, at the left. Bill Beaudry was next to Hauser, Philip Neill next to Banning.

John was the last to arrive; as he dropped into his chair at the foot of the table a flood of memories washed over him. Where he had believed in a God of love, August Hauser had believed in a God of righteousness; where he had been tentative in passing judgment, August had been able to recognize impiety and affix the appropriate punishment. Nearly every issue in the community had been fought out between these extremes. Though Jonathan Waite had been a kindly man, he had been convinced that it was both wiser and safer for a congregation to live up to the letter of the religious law. Bill Beaudry's literal-minded father had agreed with Waite and Hauser, repeating that "we must avoid the very appearance of evil." Philip Neill, who liked his glass of whisky and occasionally disappeared into Los Angeles for a night of dissipation, had a fundamentalist wife, against whose fervent religious principles he dared not vote in meeting. Sympathetic Ralph Banning was a good business manager for the church but, in disputes over ethical policy, he always maintained a merchant could not afford to be outspoken. That had left John against the field, pleading for a softer and gentler religion, a more liberal attitude toward the changing world, tolerance for transgressors. Though he had frequently been outvoted by the show of hands around the table, though in the heat of argument someone might call him a heathen or a backslider, he had sometimes been able to make the God of righteousness yield to the God of love.

Maxwell Widney rose to address his board, turning the wick of the kerosene lamp a little higher. The tiny tan moles stood out sharply from his light skin.

False Witness

"We have called this special meeting because our church is in danger. When I came to Mission Valley six months ago this was a friendly community. Today it is being split by unchristian gossip and the taking of sides. If I seem angry and upset, you will perhaps forgive me."

"We like it even less than you do," said Beaudry.

"How are we going to stop it?" broke in Banning.

"I have a suggestion to offer," replied the minister. "In order to quiet the Widow Smithers, I suggest we give her fifty dollars out of our church fund."

August bolted upright in the hard chair. "An excellent idea!" he cried.

"It will give the whole affair a church burial," added Philip Neill, whose irreverent joking was a constant source of discomfort to the board.

"Cheap at half the price," agreed Beaudry, "providing it does the work."

John did not like the proposal; although the return of the money might silence the Widow Smithers, it would only provide the people with something more to talk about. However, he was eager to grasp at anything that might put the wretched scandal to rest. As president of the board, August put the proposal in the form of a motion and it passed with a unanimous show of hands.

"And now," added August quietly, "I think it would also be better for the church and the community if we punished Mary Shoemaker in some way."

A stunned and shocked look came over the faces of the members of the board. Maxwell Widney turned in bewilderment to his president; it was obvious he had come to the meeting with no such thought in mind.

"What kind of punishment do you suggest, Mr Hauser?"

"Since she has broken the Eighth Commandment, the appropriate punishment would be to take away her membership in the church."

A flat, strained silence enveloped the board room. Beaudry and the minister continued to watch August, but Banning and Neill turned to look at John. He gripped the edge of the black table with his long gnarled fingers and rose, towering above the board with the wrath of a Jeremiah.

"No one is going to convict Mary Shoemaker of breaking the Eighth Commandment until they prove her guilty," he commanded in a low, impassioned voice. "Mary is a good woman. In the fifteen years since her husband died she has lived an upright and honest life. She has worked faithfully in every house in this valley: in yours, Beaudry, and yours, Banning, and yours, Neill. You would no more have thought of hiding your valuables or money from her than from your own wife. It is a contemptible thing to attack a poor and defenseless widow in a house of God and, as God is my judge, I will fight for her with the last breath in my body."

He sat down abruptly, took off his glasses and wiped the perspiration that had gathered on the lenses. The red bloom on August's cheeks had withered under John's searing charge. No one dared speak; they all waited for August to reply. It was several moments before he found his voice.

"Then you accuse my Hilda of taking the money?"

A gasp went up. No one was more astonished than John.

"Why, August, I said no such thing."

"You implied it."

"No, no!"

"You believe the money was taken from the Smithers' flour barrel, don't you?" demanded August.

"I'm not convinced of that."

"You must believe somebody stole the money or

you wouldn't be willing for us to pay it back from the church fund."

"I agreed because I hoped it might stop the talk."

"The talk about what?"

"Why, about the money being taken."

"Aah," cried August, pushing him hard, "then you do say the money was taken?"

Flabbergasted, John said slowly, "I don't reckon I know what you're driving at."

"It's all clear enough: you say the money was stolen, but Mary Shoemaker didn't steal it. That means you accuse my daughter of stealing it."

"You're putting words into my mouth, August."

"Not at all. You know that Mary was in the Smithers' flour barrel that afternoon, you know the money is gone from the barrel, but you refuse to admit Mary took it."

Driven by August's accusing and arrogant manner, John cried:

"Your daughter was also seen coming out of the widow's house that day."

The members of the board were dumfounded; it was the first time Hilda's presence in the widow's house had been given public footing. August glared at John threateningly.

False Witness

"You claim that Mary Shoemaker did not take the money. That means you accuse my Hilda of stealing it."

"I'm not accusing Hilda, but if you insist on taking it that way, you can."

9

NEVER BEFORE had a church board meeting broken up in bitterness. By breakfast time there was hardly a family did not know that, in defending Mary, John had affirmed that Hilda had been seen coming out of the Widow Smithers' house. Once John had said it in public meeting, the ban was lifted. What had been whispers became outright talk; the semicolon gave way to the full accusing sentence. August's attempt to lay the guilt on Mary Shoemaker backfired, a considerable portion of the valley now feeling free to say Hilda had stolen the money and used it to buy the new dress.

"What I don't like about it," Norman told Margaret, "is that the case is no longer Hilda versus Mary, but Hauser versus Annister. Everybody in the valley thinks he has to side with one or the other."

"Gramp had to defend Mary."

"Of course. But I wish his defense could have steered clear of implicating Hilda."

Now that taking sides had begun in earnest, the subject of August Hauser against John Annister was brought into the full light. For eighteen years John had served as president of the congregation he founded, served until August had painstakingly accumulated enough votes to push him aside. For two full decades the farmers had brought their disputes to John to be settled without rancor or cost; then August had introduced the office of justice of the peace, covertly challenging their right to go to John when they wanted their differences adjudicated. The people of the valley loved John Annister and feared August Hauser; resentment against August for contriving to take the leadership from John's hands now found a concrete means of expression.

On Saturday evening the Martells came to visit with the Annisters. Norman's father was a plain, shy man, as comfortable to live with as an old pair of shoes; his attractive mother was a brown-haired, brown-eyed woman whose father had been a schoolteacher in Boston, and from whom Norman was said to have inherited his love for books. Margaret and Norman had been devoted to each other for so long the families felt akin.

Soon other neighbors dropped in. Herman Wolkskill arrived with Tim Temple, Herman's booming laughter almost drowning out Tim's piping voice as they mounted the front steps. Angelo Renaldi knocked at the door of his neighbor, Philip Neill, to suggest they go smoke a pipe and drink a glass of sherry with John. From up near the north pass, where the San Felice River cascaded into the valley, came the two seventy-year-old white-haired cousins, Benjamin Jenifer and James Clauves, who had been the first to join young John Annister in breaking Mission Valley to the plow. Peter Lopez and Luther Olgies hitched up the big Olgies' buckboard. The Burbanks and Gouchers, who owned the land at the south pass through which the valley people went to Los Angeles, made up a party to come. MacAdden and Wisegane, whose acres were just north of the Annister farm, walked down the riverbank, catching up with Martin Coronel and his wife, who had cut across from their house at the base of the Santa Monica range. The Hubbards and Lankershims, whose farms were in the very heart of the valley, on the road just before San Felice, brought their oldest sons. From the town itself came Hiram Hogarth, the blacksmith, Marden, owner of the stationery-and-notion store, Kearney, the druggist.

By the time Margaret brought up the jugs of cool sherry from the cellar and sliced the pound cake Mary Shoemaker had baked the afternoon before, more than forty excited neighbors had crowded into the Annister dining room, where they had met so often before to discuss community affairs: whether they should pave the road in front of the San Felice stores, the need for a schoolhouse, for a voluntary fire brigade. There were twelve dining-room chairs; the sofa, on which John sometimes took a cat nap after dinner, accommodated five; two benches from the patio gave sitting room to still eight more. John passed his big pouch of tobacco, and soon the room was filled with heavy tobacco smoke and talk about what people had been saying in town that afternoon.

"I call it a skunken thing for August to do," exclaimed Martin Coronel.

". . . trying to run poor Mary outen the church," concluded his wife, who always finished his sentences

for him, "when it's all the poor woman's got for con-
solation."

"Well, he didn't get away with it," burred Angus
MacAdden, "thanks to John, here."

"August, he like a hound after a rabbit," warned
swarthy Peter Lopez. "He never quit till he win."

"I be dogged if he win this time," said James
Clauves. "Me and Benjy was saying, coming crost the
valley, this time we ain't going to let August have his
way."

"That's what we agreed, all right," nodded Benjamin Jenifer solemnly, as though someone might
doubt Clauves.

"I was in front the Widow Smithers' cottage when
John asked Mary if she stole that money," cried Henry
Marden. "I seen the look on Mary's face when she said
no, she never seen no money and she never took no
money. No woman can look like that when she tells
a lie."

"Hell's bells, we all know Hilda took the money,"
swore burly Jerry Goucher. "Do we need the proof
to jump up and bite off the end of our nose?"

"Oh, that Hilda girl stole the money, right enough,"
observed Mrs Coronel, choosing from Margaret's plat-
ter the piece of pound cake with the most raisins in it.

"She been trying for five months to get a proposal outen the minister, and she figured the new dress would turn the trick."

"Which it certainly done," said Wisegane, blowing out his words on a sheet of smoke.

The room quieted for a moment, then Martin Olgies said heavily, "We'll fight August with you, John."

Tim Temple jumped up from the sofa.

"Tell you what we'll do," he exclaimed. "If August makes one more move to convict Mary Shoe, we'll hold open court right here in this room. John 'll be our judge like he used to be. Then we'll bring in witnesses, Ross, the manager of the Bon Marché . . . This time we'll give Hauser a run for his money . . ."

John sat at the head of his table, his cold pipe cemented between his teeth. They waited for him to speak.

"We're not thinking right, friends," he said in a low voice. "True, maybe, but not right. August's our neighbor and he's in trouble, bad. When a man's in bad trouble he don't care who he pulls down so long as he can save himself. We won't let August hurt Mary Shoe, but we won't try to hurt him, neither. I want you all to promise to do something for me."

"Sure, John. You know we will. What is it?"

"Put it out of your mind someone stole the money, that if Mary Shoe didn't, Hilda had to. We don't know the Widow Smithers had the money. We don't know maybe she lost it or spent it or somebody else took it. It's only Christian to give the benefit of doubt. If we hurt the Hausers we hurt the valley, and if we hurt the valley we hurt ourselves."

"August Hauser never reckoned thataway," broke in white-haired James Clauves. "He's hurten us aplenty to help himself."

"It still wouldn't make it right for us to hurten him," John replied directly to Clauves. "I ask it of you for old times' sake—put the whole thing out your mind; don't think about it, don't talk about it, don't try to figure if there was money or who stole it or why. Just remember nobody saw them ten-dollar bills, so nothing can be proved against nobody!"

The silence hummed while the neighbors chewed on John's thoughts and tasted their flavor. Norman Martell's father spoke first.

"We'll do it your way, John. It's no more 'n right we should."

"But we wanted you to know we're on your side," said Olgies.

"There 'll be no fight if you'll all help me settle it peaceful," replied John.

False Witness

"Ten o'clock," announced Hogarth, jamming his leather-fobbed watch back into the narrow top pocket of his overalls. "Time to be driving toward home and bed. We got to be up early to scrub for church."

When the last of his company had gone, John took the Bible off the open-faced sideboard and began reading in the gospels to tranquilize his spirit. Margaret and Norman left the smoke-drenched room, going out the front door into the clean-smelling night. Their arms lightly about each other's waist, they walked across the lawn to the oak. Suddenly a figure loomed out of the darkness beyond the low fieldstone fence.

"Who's there?" called Margaret.

"It's me, Mrs Hauser. May I come in?"

"Why, Mrs Hauser, of course." She ran to open the gate. "Are you alone . . . so late at night?"

"Yes, I . . . I've been waiting . . . until your friends left. Your grandfather hasn't gone to bed yet?"

Surprised, she answered slowly, "No, I don't believe so."

While Norman led Mrs Hauser into the dark parlor and lit the gold glass lamp, Margaret went to summon her grandfather, who paused only long enough to lock his Bible and take off his spectacles. Mrs Hauser was pacing the floor, a pale, drably dressed woman of forty-nine who looked as old as John. When Margaret started to leave the room, Mrs Hauser put out a hand to detain her.

"Please don't go, Margaret. I want a woman to hear what I have to say. No, you stay too, Norman; you're a lawyer, maybe you can help."

"Then let us all sit down," said John.

Mrs Hauser crowded forward on the edge of a rocker.

"People are saying my daughter stole the Widow Smithers' money to buy a new dress!"

"No, they . . ."

"I know what they are saying," she persisted. "But it isn't true."

"August gave her the money?" asked John eagerly.

"No, August didn't."

"Then where did she get it?"

"From me. I gave it to her." She jumped to her feet, her body quivering. "It was my lifetime savings. I put it together out of nickels and pennies. Almost thirty years it took me to save fifty dollars! And now they accuse my daughter of stealing it."

She sat down abruptly, crying into her locked fingers. After a moment she raised her head again, her pupils swimming.

False Witness

"You can't know what I've suffered! Never to have a dollar to call your own, never to be able to go into a store and buy something . . . to have your husband buy everything . . . to have to beg for decent clothes for yourself and your little girl . . . If not for Hilda, I would have killed myself long ago."

"Mrs Hauser, please."

"It's the truth. I stood it only for her sake. John, you remember when I first came into this valley. I was pretty, wasn't I? With blonde hair like Hilda's? I liked to laugh and have fun, didn't I? He crushed all those things out of me. . . . But I vowed he wouldn't do that to my daughter! I taught her to stand up against her father, to live her own way, to be happy while she could . . ."

She went to the front window and stared into the darkness.

"Since the first year I came to Mission Valley I've been trying to save enough money to run away. I lied, I played tricks; I even fell so low I stole pennies from his lockbox when he was asleep. Sometimes weeks went by when I couldn't add a dime to my savings. Think of it, to work thirty years to collect fifty dollars . . . not even two dollars a year. Then I saw I'd never get together enough money to run away"—she turned her face bravely to her listeners—"so I decided to save to help my daughter get away when her chance came. When she fell in love with the minister, I knew the time had come. I begged August to give her the money for a new dress. Hilda begged him. But he thought we were crazy to want to spend fifty dollars on clothes."

She turned to look out the window again. When she spoke it was the barest whisper. "I gave Hilda my fifty dollars, all I had to show for thirty years of keeping house for August Hauser."

She walked quickly to the long console table, stood leaning on it opposite John.

"That's where she got the money, John, from her own mother. You've got to believe me!"

"I do believe you," he replied.

"Thank God! And you'll do something to help me?"

"Anything you ask."

"Tell the valley where she got the money! Tell the people her own mother gave it to her. Tell them I gave her my life savings so she could buy a pretty dress and marry the minister."

"I'll tell them, Mrs Hauser," he promised.

Norman had been trying hard to keep his thoughts

from being immersed in emotional pity for Mrs Hauser. He rose and went to her.

"Don't do this," he said firmly.

"Don't . . . ?"

"You will only hurt your daughter."

"Why . . . why will it hurt her?"

"As things stand now, no one can say for sure August didn't give her the money. If you allow this story to get out, it will be proof. Then they'll say August was frightened, that he put you up to it."

"But he didn't . . . he doesn't even know I'm here. . . ."

"People won't believe that; they'll think you're taking desperate measures to defend your daughter. I'm afraid you will be getting her in deeper than before."

Mrs Hauser clenched her hand against her breast while she stared at Norman.

"I would think that Norman is right," said Margaret when her grandfather's eyes sought hers. To Mrs Hauser she added comfortingly, "My grandfather has just asked his friends not to take sides in this affair and not to talk about it any more. Instead of adding new complications, if we can only let it die down . . ."

Mrs Hauser took John's hand and washed it hysterically between her sweating palms.

"You won't listen to them, John. You'll do this for me; you'll help me to protect my daughter? You've always been so kind, you won't refuse me now?"

John soothed her as best he could.

"I'll do like you ask, Mrs Hauser. Norman's a good reasoner, but reasoning don't count in the face of what you're suffering."

10

THOUGH AUGUST HAUSER had kept his wife too secluded in their brown shingled house at the south pass of the river for her neighbors ever to know or love her, they had always felt sympathy for her plight. When John kept his promise to retell the mother's story, it seemed as though Mrs Hauser's confession had been just the heroic gesture needed to save her daughter. Realizing that a family tragedy lay implicit in the situation, Mission Valley reduced its rehearsing of the Widow Smithers' case to shamed undertones. Then, after a three-day smothered calm, the new fuel suddenly caught fire and the community burst into flame again. Everyone pitied Mrs Hauser; few believed her.

False Witness

"Save fifty dollars that August don't know about," snorted Mrs Clauves. "She couldn't save fifty cents!"

"But I don't blame her for telling it," added Mrs Jenifer. "I'd do as much for my daughter."

Up to this moment it had been necessary to interject into every discussion, "August may have given Hilda that money; after all, the daughter of a rich man doesn't have to steal." Mrs Hauser having swept away that line of defense, the problem had simplified itself: either Mrs Hauser was telling the truth, in which case Hilda might be innocent, or Mrs Hauser was lying, in which event her daughter was most certainly guilty.

This dilemma was argued a thousand times over in every home and every group that met. Mrs Hamil, who would have served as the community newspaper if not for the strictures of the Annister plaque, flowered into the most important personage in the valley, a liaison officer dashing breathlessly from one house to another with new clues, facts, fancies, theories and suppositions, giving to the Widow Smithers' story the drama of the magazine serials with which she had contented herself during the lean years. Through her unflagging efforts every person in Mission Valley knew what every other person had to say about the case; like a bee in the springtime, she impregnated each new discussion on which she lighted with pollen from the last.

The one house in Mission Valley which Mrs Hamil avoided was John Annister's Mission Oaks. No one discussed the Smithers case when John was about, but from the embarrassed looks, strained hushes and fragments of sentences left dangling in mid-air when he approached, he knew his neighbors talked of little else. What distressed him even more was that the people appeared to enjoy the excitement of the gossip and friction. Even the friends who had assembled in his dining room that night to pledge him their support had broken their promise not to badger names and reputations. The fever had proved contagious; it had caught them too. Sometimes it was difficult for John to recognize his neighbors; their gentle simplicity was vanishing under his very eyes.

"Ever notice how narrow our valley looks in storm time?" he asked Margaret as they stood gazing at the lead-domed sky. "Like the land is being squeezed between the two ranges? People can be like that too."

May proved to be a turbulent month. A powdery white heat haze hovered between the mountains all day, making a man's fence the border of his world, the beauties of the valley, which had always unified its people, obliterated and forgotten. In mid-afternoon the haze blackened, lightning flashed dimly through the thick-coated air, thunder came rolling down the pockets and gullies of the Sierra Madres, while the quail and blackbirds filled the valley with their frightened complaints as they took to wing. Piercing the blackness, a stray shaft of sunlight touched now a field, now a house, like a long-burning sulphur match. Through the north pass slashed slanting streaks of gray rain, to disappear into slanting streaks of purple-furrowed earth. At dusk, having washed the haze from the air, the rain stopped, the valley reappeared in all its chordal beauty: orchards in multigreen bloom, tall lines of eucalyptus windbreaks, bright gold fields next to sea-green grass, white houses looking cleansed and damp in the late sunlight, wild lilac and jasmine exhaling their fragrance now that the heaviness was gone. Smoke drifted upward in thin streamers, vanishing into a shallow sea-green sky; the Sierra Madres emerged in such stark clarity one could reach out and touch them, four sharply defined ridges rolling and mounting backward in the sweet-smelling rain-washed air.

Sudden storms also lashed through the inhabitants of Mission Valley; quarrels broke out between neighbors who had lived at peace with each other for years on end. Tim Temple, who had endured no one knew what tortures of restraint to keep his temper from bursting out at his closest neighbor, Bill Beaudry, went into his chicken coop one morning to find that the Beaudry dog had broken loose again and killed nineteen of his prize Rhode Island Reds. Furious at Beaudry for having discharged Mary Shoemaker, thus indicting her before the entire valley, Tiny Tim no longer saw any need to restrain his temper. He stormed onto the Beaudry farm and tore into his neighbor, indifferent to the fact that Beaudry was a foot taller and a hundred pounds heavier. As Mrs Hamil recounted the story later that day, Temple and Beaudry had argued for two full hours, rehearsing their swallowed grievances of the ten years past, and had parted with bad blood between them. Up near the north pass, where the river made its entrance into the valley, James Jenifer found his newly planted string-bean patch flooded out by a break in Malcolm Shepard's clumsy irrigation ditch. For two decades the Shepard irrigation ditch had been breaking, and for two decades gentle James Jenifer had been enduring the havoc it wrought with neighborly patience. Having heard the night before that Shepard had called John Annister a busybody for butting into the Widow Smithers' affair, when it was as plain as the nose on a man's face that Mary Shoemaker had taken the money out of the flour barrel, seventy-year-old Jenifer rapped on the door of the Shepard house and, with his white mustache trembling, had demanded that Shepard replant his field or pay for the damage.

As the last agitated days of May set behind the western range, and the first Sunday in June approached, the Widow Smithers' case was thrown into sharp focus. Everyone asked himself and, subsequently, his neighbor, "Will the Reverend Mr Widney marry Hilda Hauser when she is under suspicion of theft?" No one dared ask this question of either August Hauser or the clergyman, but Hilda did her best to answer it by visiting a number of homes, telling of Widney's schoolmate who was coming out from Los Angeles to perform the ceremony, of the banquet August was serving in the community house after the ceremony, to which the entire valley was invited.

Of all the people who were perplexed over this knotty problem, no one was as troubled as Maxwell Widney himself. Dressed in a turtle-necked sweater, and with bicycle clamps holding the flaps of his trousers folded across his ankles, he bicycled into the Annister yard late on Tuesday afternoon of the second day of June, just five days before the date set for his wedding. Grace brought him into the kitchen where Margaret was crouched before the oven, ladling gravy over a roast.

"Here's Mr Widney come to call, Margaret," said her mother, flustered. "He insisted I bring him into the kitchen. I told him it wasn't polite to bring the minister into the kitchen, but just the same . . ."

"Kitchen's the nicest room in the house right this minute," replied Margaret without rising. "Could we tempt you to stay and share our leg of lamb, Mr Widney?"

"Thank you, Miss Margaret. I've just come to speak to your grandfather for a moment."

"He's in the barn, treating Mollie. Mollie's our milch cow," she explained. "She tore her leg on a rusty nail."

The barn smelled of pressed hay and medicine. When John saw the minister he put the cork back into the veterinary's bottle, washed his hands in a bucket of water and dried them by rubbing his palms down the front of his shirt.

"Mr Annister, I'm sorely troubled," began Widney.

"I've been told a heap of troubles in my time, son."

"Well, then . . . I want to tell you I'm going to . . . resign from the church."

"But why? You're doing your job fine here."

Widney stood with his head bowed, unwilling to answer.

"I . . . I don't think it's fair to the church under the circumstances . . . to marry and stay on . . ."

"You must love Hilda very much to do this for her."

Widney looked up, a fine light on his face.

"She has all the qualities I had always hoped for in a wife: she has high spirits, she likes to laugh and have fun."

"Then marry your Hilda and forget all thought of resigning."

"But the talk . . . ?"

". . . will die down as soon as she is your wife."

Widney thought hard, the tiny tan moles shining.

"I begged Mr Hauser to postpone the wedding for a couple of weeks. He won't hear of it. He says if I don't marry Hilda this Sunday, I convict her of the crime. That's why I prefer to marry her and then resign."

"Your resigning will hurt her even worse," said John thoughtfully. "Folks hereabout might think you were afraid to come back."

"You think that if the wedding is postponed, we can clear this up?"

"I'm sure we can, son."

"Then I'm going to the Hausers immediately to tell them so."

11

John slept little that night for thinking of the tempest that would be unleashed in the morning, when Maxwell Widney announced the postponement of the wedding. To his surprise, no such announcement was made. He heard instead that Ira Barkley, who managed August Hauser's business office, had devised a solution for the problem. Ira proposed that Mary Shoemaker and Hilda Hauser each be given an envelope addressed to the widow, that the one who had the fifty dollars was to put the money in the envelope and return it through the mail, thus closing the incident once and for all.

Ira Barkley was a sick man, with thin discolored hair and a yellowish shrunken face that made it difficult to tell whether he was forty or sixty. Only in work could he forget the pain that constantly attended him. August had found him in a grain merchant's office in Los Angeles six years before and had been attracted by Ira's capacity for work. He followed August around with doglike devotion, kept his books and files, answered his mail, collected his accounts; in addition, he took charge of August's official business: recording of births, marriages and deaths, keeping records of land ownership and taxes, distributing the mail.

Barkley first offered his suggestion of the two envelopes over the front counter of Banning's general merchandise store, then at Kearney's drugstore and last to a group of women selecting paper doilies at Marden's. After the first gasping surprise, the village met his proposal with indifference: the community was now enjoying the dramatic flavor of the scandal.

John Annister rejected the idea more bluntly than anyone else when Ira Barkley walked the two miles to Mission Oaks that evening. As Ira perched on a rocker in the parlor, his scrawny neck rising out of the yellowing celluloid collar with its black shoestring tie, looking as though the next breath of air might snuff out his tiny flame of life, John remembered what Tim

Temple had once observed: "August keeps so much work piled up for Ira, the poor devil can't find time to die. Maybe that's why he loves August so much."

"No, thanks, no sherry," he said in a tight-lipped voice as Margaret brought in the decanter from the sideboard. "I just finished my bowl of crackers and milk. . . . Why don't you think it's a good idea, John? Can't be much doubt whichever woman took the money 'd like to return it worst way. This 'll give 'em a chance. Widow 'll have her money back, and nobody 'll know who took it."

"And nobody 'll ever stop wondering who took it," replied John grimly. "It's like Norman warned us about Mrs Hauser: if you want a fire to go out, you don't throw more wood on it. It's not important we find out who stole that consarned money, if anybody did; but it's mighty important we stop our talk. Gossip breeds hate, and nothing grows on hate but more hate."

"You won't be angry with me, John, if I propose it to the minister?"

"You'd be better off home in bed."

"I can't go to bed yet," replied Ira, rising with a palm stretched out flat over his stomach. "My ulcers don't stop smarting till almost midnight."

False Witness

Early the next morning Mary Shoemaker came running up the river path, terror masking her usually immobile face.

"Mr John, why did you send for me?"

Puzzled, John asked, "Send for you? I didn't . . ."

"I mean the church board. What are they going to do to me now?"

"You must be mistaken. The board hasn't sent for you."

"Ira Barkley stopped to home last night, said the board wanted to see me. Mr John, what are they going to do to me?"

"Now, now, Mary, calm yourself. You know I won't let anything happen to you. Come back to have supper with us; if I hear there's a meeting, we'll go up together."

Word reached John during the noon hour that he was wanted at a special board meeting that night. After Mary had eaten her supper on the little table in the kitchen and John had donned his second-best suit, they set out for the church, entering the little board room from the rear. Hilda Hauser, dressed in a black tailored suit with a white lingerie shirtwaist, was seated between her father and Maxwell Widney. She nodded sedately to John and Mary, her face lovelier than ever in its unaccustomed seriousness. Mary Shoemaker stiffened when she saw Hilda, then seated herself at the end of the table next to John, frightened half out of her wits.

After a pause Maxwell Widney rose with obvious reluctance to open the meeting. He talked directly to John.

"Last evening Mr Ira Barkley came to my house with a suggestion for the settlement of the Smithers affair. Feeling I had no authority in the matter, I sent him to Mr Hauser."

He sat down abruptly, turning the meeting over to August by gesture rather than word. August climbed ponderously to his feet.

"I thought Barkley's suggestion might have something to it," he said, "so we got in my buggy and went to see Ralph Banning, Bill Beaudry and Philip Neill. They thought the plan might work, so we called this meeting to propose it to the two women."

"Why wasn't notice sent that the board was considering this idea?" demanded John, half rising. "How could the board decide to do anything when it hadn't been called together to vote?"

"We had a majority in favor of it," replied August, "even if you voted no."

"That's not proper procedure," barked John. "It's not town-meeting methods."

"Saves time," replied August, running his hand vigorously over the stubble on the back of his egg-shaped head. "We got to get this nuisance settled right now."

"All I said, John," interpolated Neill, "was that it was all right by me if it was all right by the board."

"Ira Barkley's waiting in the church," said Banning, who shied away from friction like a skittish horse from blown paper. "Can't hurt nothing to let him suggest, can it, John?"

"You've gone this far without asking my opinion," John replied to no one in particular. "Looks like I wouldn't be in a position to stop you going the rest of the way."

Banning opened the vestry door to the church and called. Ira Barkley came in. He had put on a clean white celluloid collar for the occasion. He stood beside the minister and drew forth two stamped envelopes from inside his blue pin-striped coat. His nervousness made him speak in a pompous manner, as though he were delivering a well-rehearsed oration.

"I hold in my hand two identical envelopes addressed to the Widow Smithers. I propose Mary Shoemaker and Hilda Hauser each take an envelope, and the one stole the money put it in the envelope and mail it back to the widow. No one will ever know who mailed the envelope."

The mottled red-and-white flush that had begun at Mary's rough-skinned bosom radiated upward to the roots of her hair.

"I never stole no money," she cried. "I got nothing to return."

John thumped his fist on the church table in anything but an ecclesiastical fashion.

"Right as rain!" he exclaimed.

"Then you refuse to accept the envelope?" asked Hauser.

"Do I have to take it, Mr John?" Mary pleaded.

"You certainly do not. This board has no right to force an innocent person through such a humiliating act."

"Then I refuse," said Mary stoutly.

"What about you, Hilda?" Beaudry asked from across the table. "Are you willing to take an envelope?"

"Yes, I'll take one," answered Hilda quickly. "I didn't steal the money, so there's no reason why I shouldn't take an envelope."

Dimly, in the accusing silence that followed, Mary sensed she had been tricked. As all eyes turned upon her, she lowered her head.

"What should I do, Mr John?" she murmured.

John took off his spectacles and shut them into their black cardboard case with a protesting bang. Divested of his robe of office, he allowed himself to perceive that Hilda had been told in advance of the purpose of this meeting, that a trap had been set for the slow-thinking Mary. If Mary refused to take an envelope, the story would go out that Hilda had willingly accepted one and hence must be innocent, that Mary had refused and hence must be guilty. The whole affair smelled to him of sharp dealing, an odor he never thought would permeate his board room.

"I reckon you better take an envelope, Mary," he said with disgust. "Looks like you haven't got much free choice."

"If you tell me to, Mr John."

"The envelopes are identical, as you can see," said Barkley, holding them out toward Hilda. "Take whichever one you want; it don't make a mite of difference."

"I'll take this one," said Hilda.

117

False Witness

Ira Barkley walked the length of the table, handing the second envelope to Mary. She held it with the tips of her fingers.

"Then it's understood," said Barkley, extracting the last ounce of juice from his hour of importance. "The one has the fifty dollars puts it in the envelope and mails it tonight."

There was only one way to post a letter in Mission Valley, by dropping it in the slot in the narrow sector of the building August Hauser leased to the government. Since no one slept in the single block of stores in San Felice, it was not possible to watch the post office all night; but there were houses lining the road on both sides of town and from their front windows the vigil was faithfully kept. Mrs Kearney's lasted until two o'clock on the west approach; Mrs Marden's until three-thirty on the east.

When Mission Valley climbed out of its bed at six o'clock the next morning, the first question asked was, "Did Mary or Hilda go to the post office last night?" By breakfast everyone knew that, after eight o'clock the evening before, no one had entered the village from either direction, and consequently no letter could have been mailed. The skepticism that had been felt the day before was loudly expressed.

False Witness

"Only a bookkeeping idiot like Ira Barkley would think of such a lunatic idea," said Mrs Kearney.

"Course it wouldn't work. They'd know somebody'd see 'em mailing the letter," concluded Mrs Coronel.

In spite of the conviction that the plan had failed, an even larger crowd jammed into the post office than assembled there the day before Christmas. All the townspeople were collected, as well as a number of farmer families who used the day's marketing as an excuse to be on the ground. At a quarter to ten the Widow Smithers entered the village wearing her white wedding gown, turned a rich yellow to match the straw hat perched on the back of her head. The crowd on the sidewalk parted to make way for her; a rolling murmur preceded her into the post office, "Here's the Widow Smithers." She placed herself in front of the brown metal boxes behind which Ira Barkley was sorting the mail, retelling the story of the fifty dollars, her set of false teeth, inserted in honor of the occasion, chattering a staccato accompaniment at the one corner where they met.

As ten o'clock approached the people became still and tense. The widow stopped to turn her face toward the wall of metal discs. Everyone knew Ira Barkley's stamped envelope could not be there, yet so many fantastic things had been happening, they had come to believe nothing impossible.

On the very stroke of ten the single stamp window was thrown open. Ira stuck out his thin face, gazed at the crowd for a moment in dramatic silence, then cried, "The mail is up!"

No one opened his box. Even the widow, who had been waiting with so much anxiety and hope, could not bring herself to move. Someone called, "Go ahead, Widow Smithers, see what you got in the grab bag." Only then did she reach up a hand covered with brown senile spots to open her box.

"Look," cried Mrs Kearney in an awe-struck tone that could be heard clear out to the sidewalk. "She's got a letter!"

The widow's hand trembled so hard she dropped the envelope to the floor. Ralph Banning picked it up. Tears filled the old woman's eyes.

"Open it for me, Ralph," she said. "I can't see."

Banning tore from the envelope a thin ragged strip, blew into it to belly its sides, then emptied the contents into the widow's shaking palms. Slowly, one after the other, five ten-dollar greenbacks appeared. There was one last moment of stunned silence, then everybody began talking at once. Over the boil of voices could be heard the shrill cry of the widow.

"I told you I had the money! I told you it was stolen from me; I told you so!"

} 12 {

LITTLE WORK WAS DONE in Mission Valley that day.
Until the existence of the money had been established,
no one could prove the existence of a theft. Now that
the thief had returned the loot, the community was
saddled with a crime that had to be solved if it was to
live at peace again. Though it was Thursday, a meeting was called of the Tuesday afternoon coffee club.
Many an industrious farmer let the hours slip by telling his neighbors he couldn't understand such goings
on, and for land's sake, who did steal that money, anyway? A hysteria of speculation seized the valley, a
hysteria as contagious as though it were spread from
mouth to mouth by a communicable germ.

False Witness

When plump and pretty Mrs Wolkskill arrived with the news that morning, Mary Shoemaker was on her hands and knees scrubbing the Annister kitchen floor.

"I think we'd better let Gramp tell Mary," said Margaret, as she called to her mother to come and say hello to Mrs Wolkskill. "I'll sound the gong for him; he went off this morning without eating breakfast or telling us where he was going to work."

The bell's deep mellow tones rang through the clear dry sunlight. Soon they saw John's tall lean figure in fading blue overalls and blue shirt swinging through the alfalfa furrows, the warm flesh colors of his hands and face standing out sharply against the spring green of his fields. Margaret ran to the far end of the patio to meet him.

"The fifty dollars has been returned," said John while they were still a few steps apart.

Margaret stopped short.

"How did you know?"

"From the look on your face. And because I've been dreading all morning for that gong to ring."

"But you said last night when you came home from the board meeting that it was impossible . . . that it wouldn't be . . ."

"I got to thinking when I couldn't sleep. August was anxious the plan go through, and when August is anxious something be tried, he has the result all figured out. . . . What did Mary say?"

"We thought you ought to tell her."

Grace and Mrs Wolkskill joined them as they went into the kitchen, where Mary stood at the sink rinsing her large worn scrubbing rags.

"Mary," said John, "the Widow Smithers got back her fifty dollars in the mail this morning."

Mary turned, her face gleaming with sweat, searching the eyes of the surrounding ring.

"I'm glad," she said dully. "Now maybe they let me alone."

"I think they will," replied John quietly as she dropped onto her hands and knees and ran her soapy brush over the blue-and-white oilcloth squares. "When you come on Tuesday, bring me the envelope Ira Barkley gave you last night. I'll keep it safe for you."

Mary looked up from her position on all fours, wiped the beads of perspiration off her forehead with an upward movement of her forearm.

"I can't do that, Mr John."

"Why not?"

False Witness

"Because I burned it first thing I got home last night."

In the throttled silence that followed, no one dared look at his neighbor; Mary took up her scrubbing where she had left off.

"Why did you burn it, Mary?"

"'Tweren't no use to me, Mr John. I didn't have no stolen money to put in it. I hated the very touch of it, like it was a accusation 'gainst me. So when I lit my fire in the grate, I threw in the envelope first thing."

John's eyes darkened as they always did when he was troubled.

"There wasn't no one there saw you burn it, Mary?"

"There wouldn't be nobody in my house to see me, Mr John."

"Well, you had every right to burn it." He walked to the sink, took the tin cup from the window ledge and turned on the tap. "Only I sure wish you hadn't," he said before drinking.

Running footsteps echoed through the house as Tim Temple burst into the kitchen, his face as flaming red as his hair.

"John, my wife just came back from the village . . ."

"The widow's got her money," interrupted John.

"No, no, I mean what's just happening, just now." He spoke with a slow up-and-down movement of the head. "Hilda Hauser's been going from store to store, showing the envelope she took from Ira Barkley last night!"

Tim's gaze traveled from face to face; instead of explanation he found only bewilderment.

"John, you'd better drive Mary into town," he continued when no one spoke, "so she can show her envelope too."

"I can't do that, Tim," John replied with a touch of despair. "Mary hasn't got her envelope. She says she burned it first thing she got home last night."

Mary bulked before Tim.

"That's right, Mr Temple," she said without show of emotion. "I ain't got no envelope to tote from store to store."

By nightfall sentiment had swung sharply against Mary Shoemaker. She could not show the Barkley envelope as proof of her innocence and, after all, she had been in the flour barrel, hadn't she?

When Norman arrived from Los Angeles at seven that evening, he found the Annister household in a state of dejection.

False Witness

"Oh, Norm, I'm glad you've come," Margaret whispered, holding her cheek against his for a brief moment. "Gramp is so upset we hardly know where to turn next."

John was sitting at his usual place at the head of the table, reading his Bible, the spectacles low on his nose. Norman slid an arm affectionately about the older man's shoulder, then hitched up a chair and plunged without preliminaries into the problem.

"Look, Gramp," he said in a coolly objective manner, "the fact that Hilda has an envelope addressed to the Widow Smithers means nothing. If Ira Barkley could prepare two such envelopes, he could prepare a hundred."

John closed his Bible, snapped the lock and took off his glasses. While one part of his mind had been reading Scripture, the other part had been thrashing his problem on the cold stone of facts. Could he be mistaken about Mary Shoemaker? She had been in the flour barrel—she needed money—she had been unwilling to accept one of Ira Barkley's envelopes—and now her envelope was gone. But if you couldn't judge by character, by what could you judge? How could an honest woman steal from a helpless old widow? If Mary Shoemaker was a thief, then nothing was understandable, neither in the heavens nor on earth. No, it was unthinkable!

"It may not mean anything to us, son, but it does to the valley. They got Mary convicted already . . . particular since she can't show her envelope. We're in a terrible muddle."

"If only," said Norman meditatively, "we could get a look at the five greenbacks the Widow Smithers received in her envelope."

"What good would that do, Norm?" asked Margaret.

"The widow claims her bills were kept on the bottom of that flour barrel for fifteen years. It should be easy to find out whether these are the same bills or different ones. If they are the same bills, then obviously Hilda could not have bought her new dress with them . . ."

"Good," John nodded. "If Hilda is innocent, we've found a way to clear her. Let's take the buggy and go into San Felice."

The Widow Smithers generally retired before dark, but tonight, when John pulled up his mare, they found a lamp burning in her window. Through the darkness came the whinny of other horses. A dozen neighbors were crowded into the widow's small parlor, taking quick turns at the talk: the Kearneys, Mardens and O'Melvanys from the village, the Neills, Mahlers, Hamils and Renaldis from neighboring farms. The widow's face was bright with pleasure, both at having gotten her money back and at being the center of attention.

"You see, it's proved, John Annister," she cried, pointing to the five greenbacks on the center table. "You told me to prove I had the money, and now it's proved."

"Could we look at that money?" asked John.

The old woman grabbed up her bills and shrank away from him.

"I'm not going to let you take it away from me. I'm not going to lose it again."

"Nobody wants to take your money away from you," John answered patiently. "We merely want to look at it for a minute."

Cautiously the widow tendered the five bills. John passed one to Norman, another to Margaret.

"How long did you say you had this money?" asked Norman in a conversational tone.

"Fifteen years, since Smithers died."

"How long did he have them before that?"

"I don't know. He kept 'em hid. He never told me."

False Witness

"In the last few years before Smithers died, would he have had any way of earning fifty dollars without you knowing about it?"

The widow chewed her underlip between her gums.

"We was awful hard put," she decided. "Smithers scraping just a few dollars a week."

"Then it's safe to assume," Norman continued, "that the ten-dollar bills were at least eighteen or twenty years old?"

The widow stared at him without answering.

"This bill I'm holding ain't no twenty years old," announced Philip Neill, who had taken a greenback from John. "It's no more 'n two or three years old."

He passed it to Mahler on his right, who tapped it with the wet stem of his pipe and said, "By Joe, this bill on the bottom of a flour barrel no twenty years never sat."

After waiting for several moments for the excited hubbub to quiet, John turned again to the widow.

"Widow Smithers, you told us you used to take the money out of the flour barrel every day and count it. Is this the same money you used to count?"

The widow held out her hand. The bills were placed in it. She stood rubbing them, feeling their texture with her thumb, running her finger across their oblong surface, then looked up with a scowl.

"This ain't the money I found in Smithers' trunk," she announced in a tremolo. "It ain't wrinkled and rough enough. It ain't folded like I kept my money folded, in a tight ball."

When no one spoke, Kearney looked at John and asked, "What does it all mean?" John nodded at Norman.

"Before we came in here," replied Norman, "you were saying that since Hilda Hauser still has her envelope, and Mary Shoe hasn't, Mary Shoe must have returned the money. But if Mary Shoe returned it, why didn't she return the original bills? She hasn't been out of Mission Valley since the money disappeared, so she couldn't have spent it, nor could she have spent it in Mission Valley without all you folks knowing about it."

"What I don't savvy," said Henry Marden with a frown, "is where Mary coulda got hold of five different bills between the board meeting last night and the early mail this morning?"

"Unless she had them saved up at home?" proffered Mrs O'Melvany.

Mrs Kearney waved a dismissing hand at Mrs O'Melvany.

"How could Mary Shoe save fifty dollars on a two-dollar-a-day wage, what with taxes and upkeep on her farm . . . ?"

"It's not likely she'd be having 'em on hand the very night she needed them, and ten-dollar bills at that, even if she did save that much money."

When they reached home they found August Hauser sitting on the wooden bench under the oak, sunk into his heavy overcoat. He rose quickly and started to speak but, when he saw Margaret and Norman, stopped himself.

"Come in, August," said John.

He led him into the dining room where the lamp was still burning. August leaned across the table, gripping its edges with taut hands.

"John, what are you trying to do to us?" he asked in the low pleading voice John had heard him use only once before, in Albert Ross's front yard the day Hilda had become implicated.

"Only trying to keep an innocent woman from being convicted of a crime."

"Mrs Hamil just drove by to tell me you had been to the Widow Smithers' house to inspect the five greenbacks."

"News travels fast these days."

False Witness

"But why did you do it, John?"

"Hilda went through town this morning showing everyone an envelope addressed to the widow to prove she didn't send the money back. That convicted Mary Shoe. I had to prove that Mary didn't send the money back either."

August closed his eyes and began swaying a trifle.

"Mind if I sit? And could I have a little water to down these pills? I been feeling pretty bad the past few days . . . my heart . . ."

"I'm sorry to hear that, August. I'll get the water."

After August had swallowed his capsules and washed them down, he sat with his eyes closed. When he opened them to look at John, they were clouded and confused.

"John, Mission Valley must mean more to you than to any of the rest of us. You founded it . . . you helped create it . . . you know every tree and furrow, every inch of road and river and ditch. How can you work to destroy it?"

John lit his pipe, cupped the bowl to make it glow, then leaned across the table toward the president of his board.

"One reason I've loved this tiny corner of the earth so much is that we've all lived here in harmony . . .

with nature and with each other. We built up our good and beautiful world without lies or tricks."

August had not been listening; he had been formulating his inner resolves.

"Why can't you let Mary Shoe take the blame for this affair?" he cried. "She's only one person; nobody loves her or cares anything about her. She has no family or obligations; there will be no home broken up, no enemies made."

"Nobody loves her, August? In God's eyes the least of us is as important . . ."

"But she's only a scrubwoman," August broke in, "a cow. She has no feelings; she's too stupid to suffer the way you and I do."

John saw that August was indeed suffering; it enabled him to reply quietly.

"She is no cow. She is a human being with a full set of feelings. When she suffers it hurts her as much as it hurts you or me."

"But I wouldn't let her be hurt," August cried eagerly. "I'll see that she's fixed up."

Wonderingly, John repeated, "Fixed up?"

"Of course! I'll send her away on a vacation . . . give her a job when she comes back . . . see that she is provided for."

False Witness

"August, I refuse to have that poor woman offered as a sacrifice!"

"You'd rather sacrifice our community!"

"The only way our valley can be saved is by the truth. If we are so mean that we'd deliberately punish an innocent woman . . ."

". . . she isn't innocent, she's guilty!"

". . . to protect ourselves, then the community we have built here is ruined. Nothing good can come out of injustice. The Bible says so."

"Justice means the greatest good for the greatest number. It isn't fair to sacrifice forty years of work and five hundred people . . ."

John rose to his full height, fire in his eyes.

"Years ain't important, August. Only love is important, love and justice."

August helped himself up from the table by pushing on his hands.

"Then you insist on persecuting my Hilda."

"No, no, August. It's only when you do something to prove Mary guilty that you force me to do something to prove she's innocent."

August's face hardened.

"John, you are the one who's going to be hurt by all this."

"What could hurt me?"

"Several things . . . It was your statement at the board meeting that started people talking against Hilda. Maxwell Widney promised to wait until tomorrow morning before announcing that the marriage is to be postponed. I'm going to give you until tomorrow morning."

"To do what, August?"

"To tell Mission Valley you're sure Hilda is innocent."

"If I do that, now the money has been returned, I convict Mary Shoe."

"John, do it for my sake. Declare Hilda innocent. Then Widney will go through with the wedding on Sunday. Save my daughter from the disgrace you've let her in for."

"I can't do that, August."

"Very well, then I shall take action against you."

"Action? Against me?"

"Yes. I shall go into Los Angeles in the morning and order my lawyer to bring suit against you for slander!"

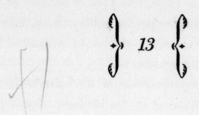

13

EARLY THE NEXT MORNING Hilda Hauser, her eyes puffed from crying, called at Marden's to ask him to hold up her order of favors and decorations because she had decided to postpone her wedding. A valley-wide split developed at once over the Reverend Mr Maxwell Widney. He was accused of weakness in the face of a difficult situation, praised for his courage in defying August Hauser; he was condemned for his caddishness in jilting Hilda, lauded for his devotion to the best interests of the church. More and more families were plunged into argument over the Widow Smithers' case.

"August was wrought up last night when he did his

threatening," said John, with a quick intake of breath when he heard that Hauser had spent the day at his roll-top desk, nodding to people as they sauntered past to see how he was taking the postponement. "He would never file suit against me."

As he approached the door of his barn he found Jerry Goucher squatting in the sunlight, chewing a thick piece of straw. Jerry was a brute of a man with a burly torso; he was not very bright but he would work his heart out for a neighbor in distress.

"John, you got a ax around handy?"

"In the woodshed."

"Would you do me something with it?"

"Sure. What?"

"Split my blockhead open. I've gone skunken weasel."

John remained silent, watching Jerry wrinkle the narrow field of skin between his bushy black eyebrows and low hairline.

"I'm three years owing in my taxes." He spat out a piece of straw in disgust. "You know how it is, John, a man gets his money from a crop, he means to pay them goldarned taxes, but there's things he's been waiting for all year; the missus and kids, they got a list of wants long as a pitchfork handle. A man buys a few things first, always meaning to pay them taxes, but soon they ain't no money left, and he figures the county don't need the money, leastaways not half as bad as he does, and he keeps hoping maybe they'll forget him . . ."

"Then what makes you worried so all of a sudden?"

"August—he sent word with Ira Barkley this morning—claims the county wants me to pay or get out." He rose from the squatting position, clenched a hand over each hard bicep, then tore his arms loose as though breaking apart a tightly wound rope. "I ain't so mean," he blurted, "I wouldn't come confess what I'm agonna do. . . . From now on I'm saying Hilda Hauser be innocent and Mary Shoe stole that money."

"You don't believe that."

"I ain't saying I believe it. I'm saying I'm saying it."

He slapped John roughly on the shoulder, turned away and headed north along the river. John stood numbed, able to distill no clear feeling but pain from his clashing thoughts. After a few moments he knew what he must do: confront August and persuade him to give up this coercing of his neighbors. He hitched up the mare and made for town. The first stand of honey-colored hay had been cut and piled in rhythmical intersecting rows across the yellow stubble fields, a scene he always enjoyed, but today he could see before him only the rage-contorted face of August Hauser as he had seen it the night before in his dining room.

As Kearney's drugstore appeared down the road, and he slowed the mare from her trot, his mind cleared; he realized that if he accused August of intimidating Jerry Goucher, August would descend in his full wrath upon Jerry. . . . The reins dropped from his fingers; the mare made her way to the hitching post in front of Marden's and turned to gaze at her master in curiosity when he continued to sit motionless upon the high seat.

Almost without knowing what he did, John climbed down and pushed open the door of the store. Henry Marden came out from the back of the shop, wiping his hands on his printer's apron. Henry loved most his printing press and was forever working at it. He was a man with a secret vice: he wrote poetry, setting up his verses first in Jenson, then Scotch Roman, then Granjon, to see in which type his rhymes looked best. Since he was rarely able to get all the ink off his hands, everything bought at Marden's carried the unmistakable label of his fingerprints. Always he carried a dream in his eye; today that dream was a sad one.

False Witness

"What's troubling you, Henry? Printing press break down?"

"No. I was just wondering where I could move it."

"What's the matter with where it is?"

"It doesn't look like it can stay there much longer." He sat on the edge of a stationery counter, with one leg dangling. "Seems there's a fellow in Los Angeles wants to open a business out here, will pay more rent than I can afford. I'm not a good businessman, John, you know that; salesmen make me buy stock that people in Mission Valley wouldn't have for the asking. Besides, I guess I tinker with that printing press too much instead of concentrating on my trade. I made a living for Ma and the kids all these years, but I never did save enough to build me a store of my own. The few dollars I have are tied up in this stock on the shelves."

John felt the breath contract in his chest.

"Who told you about this Los Angeles fellow wanting to rent your store?"

"August did."

"Is that all August talked to you about, Henry?"

Marden flushed. "Isn't that enough for one day?"

"Didn't he talk about the Widow Smithers' fifty dollars?"

"Well . . . come to think about it . . ."

"What did he say?"

"Wanted me to state outright who I thought took it."

"What did you answer?"

"How could I answer when I don't know? That was when he told me about having another tenant for the store."

He stood rubbing his inky hands on some waste while John hovered above him with steel gray eyes and implacable expression.

"What do you think I ought to do, John?" he murmured without looking up. "I can't go out as somebody's hired man at my age, not with Ma and the kids . . ."

The bell over the door warned them of the entrance of Mrs Sepulveda, come to buy her annual Butterick pattern for a summer dress. John bowed to Mrs Sepulveda and left the store, struck by the power August Hauser wielded in their little community. August sold most of the valley produce in Los Angeles; August brought in most of the heavy machinery on credit for the farmers; August advanced them money for their crops; August rented farms and stores . . . What didn't August do? The realization came to him that if

August could corner enough votes to push him out as head of the church he had founded, if August could foist upon the community the office of justice of the peace, for which they had neither need nor desire, then, by the very same methods, he could persuade a majority of people in the valley to make an outright statement that Mary Shoemaker was guilty.

In front of Banning's he stopped to light his pipe, the bright June sun warming his memories. Where Banning's store now stood there had been nothing but a barley field until the night of the church social, when he and Pa Beaudry, Tim Temple, James Jenifer, Hubbard, Lankershim, Shepard, Renaldi, Wisegane, Hauser and a number of other men had decided they could support a supply store of their own. They had agreed to invite the pleasant young clerk who waited on them in Glendale, Ralph Banning, to come over to Mission Valley and start a store of his own, land and building free, with a two-year guarantee of expenses. Hubbard and Lankershim had donated a strip of land on either side of the Indian trail, John had contributed the lumber, Beaudry the paint, Tim Temple and Jerry Goucher had laid out the street with their teams, Hauser had paved a block of sidewalk; every family in the valley had contributed something, whatever they could, to the beginnings of their village. With what great hopes and depth of feeling had the entire population assembled that Sunday afternoon to hear Jonathan Waite say a prayer and bless the town of San Felice as the cornerstone was laid. Nearly everything in the valley had been built with that same co-operative spirit, he ruminated, as he let the mare pick her own pace homeward; and now, more than ever, they would need their unified spirit to hold their community together.

Two days later Norman Martell drove up to Mission Oaks in a rig he had hired at the Glendale station. Margaret was fitting a new white voile dress on the form in the sewing room when he walked in.

"Why, Norm," she cried, turning quickly, "what brings you home on a Wednesday?"

"Bad news, I'm afraid." There was no mistaking the gravity beneath his attempted smile. "August Hauser filed suit yesterday against Gramp, in Hilda's name. He charges slander."

The color drained from Margaret's face. She sank onto the wooden chair, gripping one end of the seat with her hand.

"That's fantastic! Gramp hasn't hurt Hilda. August knows that. Everyone knows . . ."

False Witness

"Remember what Gramp said? 'When a man's in trouble he'll fight with any weapons that come to hand.'"

"Norman," she whispered after a pause, "I'm scared. Scared for his sake. I don't know what this will do to him."

He patted her shoulder reassuringly.

"The best way we can find out is go tell him."

They waited at the dam for John to come in from the northeast acres. It was seven o'clock before they saw him across the orchard, his hair caked with sweat, dirt stained in the lines of his face, moving effortlessly through the plowed earth, a hoe over his shoulder, his straw hat cocked to one side.

"Hello, Norman," he called from across the river. "I thought this was the middle of the week."

"It is."

"That means either good news or bad. From the look on your faces, I can tell it's bad. Give me ten minutes for a dip and I'll be able to take it better."

He undressed under the heavy oak branches, dove from the stone edge with a cake of Fairy soap in his hand, swam to the bank, where he soaped himself, and then swam back. It was only a few moments before he emerged from under the tree in a fresh gray shirt and jeans, his hair combed back wet and flat, his face gleaming. The sun setting behind the western tip of the Santa Monicas domed the valley with streaks of burnt orange, purple and indigo, brittle streaks that could be snapped between the fingers like slate.

"Gramp, August is suing you for slander and demanding ten thousand dollars damages. He appeared with his attorney to ask that the case be heard before the end of this court session."

John's face was expressionless as he gazed across the river to the Sierra Madre range, standing forth as sheer and powerful in the twilight clarity as ever did his White Mountains of New Hampshire.

"I can understand that," he said. "He wants to convince the minister of Hilda's innocence, so they can be married right away. But he hadn't ought to do a thing like this."

"We have twenty days to file our answer," Norman continued, "but if you would rather have it put over until the fall session, I'll appear before the court and make the request."

John smiled sadly while he shook his head sideways.

"I been thinking about this business ever since August made his threat, wondering what I'd feel or do if he accused me of slander before the whole world.

Now he's gone and done it, and all I can think is—he ought not show people how desperate he feels."

"At the moment, I don't share your worry over August and Hilda," cried Norman. "If you want me to . . . I'd . . . well, I'd be glad to handle the case . . ."

"Of course we want you to," exclaimed John.

". . . but I would also like your permission to bring in an older lawyer to try it with me."

"You won't need any help, son," replied John. He stepped between Margaret and Norman, took an arm of each and started back with them toward the house. "All we have to do is be honest and straightforward. As God is my judge, I have trespassed against no one. The truth will prevail."

14

THE FOLKS OF MISSION VALLEY would have been less astounded if August Hauser had filed suit against the sun for standing still in its course; to the growing community John Annister had been like an Old Testament prophet. They demanded of themselves and their neighbors, "What good can come from such a trial? How can it help Hilda? John didn't accuse her of stealing. He never said anything wrong or untrue about her." Yet deep in their thinking they were afraid.

On the Friday of the trial Mission Valley was abandoned. That morning its people had arisen at four o'clock to do their chores and drive to Glendale in time to catch the eight-o'clock train for Los Angeles. The three red plush-seated cars were jammed; half the men were obliged to stand in the aisles and guard their lunch baskets between their feet. The only family not on the train was the Hausers, August having taken his wife and daughter into Los Angeles the morning before.

· The most perturbed person was Margaret Rogers. She had spent the preceding days seething with resentment at Hauser, not only for the accusation against her grandfather, but for breaking the serenity of the valley, its tradition of living its own life within its own borders. Opposite her John gazed out the window, his blue eyes untroubled. She marveled that he could be calm when everyone else was charged with excitement. Even her mother was overwrought, folding and unfolding her now damp handkerchief between her chubby fingers.

It was only a short walk up the hot bright street to the county courthouse, a frame building set behind a green lawn and surrounded by palms. The Annisters led the way, the rest of Mission Valley trailing. They had the plain painted board courtroom to themselves. John and Margaret joined Norman inside the railing in front of the judge's dais. At five minutes to ten the

Hausers entered with their attorney, Hamilton Root, a self-assured man of about fifty, broad-beamed, with a shock of white hair waved back in a pompadour. He wore a wing collar with a black bow tie, a well-cut coat, the lapels of which were piped in black grosgrain, and suspended around his neck on the end of a black silk ribbon was a pair of glasses whose lenses folded over each other. August stared straight ahead as he walked down the center aisle to the railing and through the swinging gate; Hilda glanced from side to side with a wistful smile, but Mrs Hauser kept her face well hidden beneath a wide-brimmed straw hat. They took their places at the wooden table opposite John, Margaret and Norman; an air of tense, troubled expectancy gripped the courtroom.

At ten o'clock the door from the judge's chamber opened and the clerk of the court rose hurriedly to cry: "Hear ye, hear ye, the Circuit Court of Los Angeles County is now in session. All rise." The judge entered in his black robe, stood before his high-backed chair to bow almost imperceptibly, then sat down.

"The only matter before the court this morning," he announced, "is Hauser versus Annister. Are the parties ready?"

A jury of merchants and ranchers was quickly made

up, and Hamilton Root rose to state the case for the plaintiff.

"May it please the Court, your honor, gentlemen of the jury. The lovely young lady whom you see sitting at the table nearest to you is the plaintiff, Hilda Hauser, daughter of our eminent fellow citizen, August Hauser, a businessman and banker who, because of his integrity, has been chosen to serve his community as justice of the peace and president of his church. Miss Hauser shared her father's good reputation for honor and honesty until she became the victim of rumor, instigated and fanned, as we shall prove, by the slander uttered by the defendant, John Annister. Whether the slanderous accusations of the defendant were made by him maliciously or idly, we shall not say at this time. The evidence in that respect will speak for itself. But this the evidence will establish: that the defendant is a rancher of considerable means; that he has wielded great influence in his community, so great that the false charges have crushed this young girl and threaten to ruin her entire future. This is not a suit brought by August Hauser, who would be well able to defend himself, but by his innocent daughter, who is forced to submit herself to your mercy for vindication and the restoration of her honor."

False Witness

"Does counsel for the defense wish to make a statement?" asked the judge.

Norman began to rise, but John put a hand on his arm.

"No need to say anything now, son," he whispered. "You told me they have to prove their case. Let 'em go ahead and try; they can't prove something I didn't say."

Crouched above John, with his hands pressed hard against the edge of the table, Norman looked at the older man sternly.

"Gramp, you'll just have to let me try this case my way."

John blinked his eyelids with a tiny smile. Norman stepped to the railing of the jury box, then turned about to face the people of his valley. Everything he loved was here in this courtroom: Margaret and John watching him with confidence in their eyes; his family sitting just behind the rail, their heads held high with pride that their boy would triumph for John Annister; his friends and neighbors among whom he had grown up and whom he yearned to send back to their peaceful way of life between their two mountain ranges.

"Your honor, gentlemen of the jury. Forty years ago Mission Valley was wild and uninhabited country.

False Witness

John Annister was its pioneer; he encouraged other families to settle there; he gave them shelter in his home while he helped them clear and break the ground, plant a crop, raise a house. There is not one person in this courtroom who could not testify that he stood by them in sickness, aided them in adversity, taught them the goodness of life by his own example. He is the man who founded their Union Church and who headed it for twenty years. In the front beam of that church is embedded the very plaque of the Ninth Commandment his mother gave him when he left New Hampshire after the Civil War. He is the man to whom the entire valley brought their disputes for a just and friendly settlement. All his life he has stood for co-operation, tolerance, love of one's neighbors; above all, he has preached the virtues of the Ninth Commandment: Thou Shalt Not Bear False Witness against Thy Neighbor. Because of his example, no false witness has been borne in Mission Valley for three generations. We shall prove that John Annister uttered no slander against the plaintiff. We shall prove that if the plaintiff is crushed by what John Annister has said, it can only be because his words have been misinterpreted by a guilty conscience."

He broke off, his voice ringing with passionate sincerity. As Hamilton Root came forward to open the case for the Hausers, the judge gazed down at the scrubbed, shining faces of the spectators, sitting stiffly in their Sunday church clothes. Root called Bill Beaudry to the stand as his first witness. In honor of the occasion, Bill had made a heroic effort to shave all the beard from the crevice in his chin. Root treated Beaudry with deference.

"Mr Beaudry, you are a member of the board of the Union Church of Mission Valley?"

"I am."

"Do you remember what happened during the special Friday night board meeting?"

"Our minister called the meeting to propose returning the Widow Smithers' fifty dollars from the church funds."

"Did you vote to do so?"

"We did."

"What happened then?"

"August Hauser, president of our church, suggested that Mary Shoemaker be punished for stealing the money. John Annister reared up and said he wouldn't see Mary Shoemaker punished, because Hilda Hauser stole the money."

There was a gasp from the court, followed by a

wave of indignant whispering. The judge banged with his gavel, cutting sharply across the murmur.

"Before that Annister accusation, had anyone accused Miss Hauser of stealing the money?"

"No, never anybody."

"Thank you, Mr Beaudry. That is all."

Beaudry started to leave the witness box, but Norman stopped him.

"Mr Beaudry, you realize that any conscious twisting or misshaping of the words that came out of Mr Annister's mouth that night of the board meeting amounts to perjury?"

Root rushed forward to the dais, crying, "Your honor, I object to this attempted intimidation of the witness!"

"I'm not trying to intimidate the witness. Mr Beaudry, you realize the need to quote the accused accurately or not at all?"

"Yes, I understand," replied Beaudry.

"On the night of the board meeting, prior to the vote to pay the widow out of church funds, had anything been said about the guilt of Mary Shoemaker?"

"No."

"Had any vote been taken to ascertain whether the members thought Mary Shoemaker guilty?"

"No."

"Then August Hauser proposed solely on his own initiative that Mary Shoemaker be punished?"

"Yes."

"What did John Annister do then?"

"Defended Mary Shoemaker . . . said he wasn't going to see her punished."

"Isn't it true, Mr Beaudry, that Mr Annister did not even mention Hilda Hauser's name, that it was her own father who brought her name into the discussion?"

Beaudry rubbed his thumb in the crevice of his chin, as though he were trying to remember accurately.

"No. John Annister brought up her name."

Norman shook his head with anger.

"Isn't it true that Mr Annister denied half a dozen times during that meeting that he thought Miss Hauser guilty?"

"He said Hilda was seen coming out of the widow's house the day the money was took."

"After Albert Ross reported seeing Hilda Hauser come out of the widow's house, hadn't everybody been saying it?"

"I never heard it."

Mrs Coronel cried out, "Well, I did!" Other voices, indistinguishable in the crowd, added their agreement to this outburst. Root requested that the offending spectator be punished for contempt of court. After calling down Mrs Coronel, the judge suggested to Root that the plaintiff could have another trial before a different jury.

"I have confidence in the present jury, your honor," said Root, "and I will be satisfied with your instructing them to disregard the volunteered unsworn testimony."

It was clear to Norman that the jury was impressed by Root's attitude.

"Isn't it true that when August Hauser demanded Mary Shoemaker be excommunicated from the church, solely on the grounds that she had been in the widow's house the day the money disappeared, John Annister claimed it wasn't sufficient proof to convict her, when Hilda Hauser had also been seen coming out of the same house on the same day?"

"He said Hilda was seen coming out the widow's house. He said she was guilty."

Realizing that Beaudry would stick doggedly to his story, Norman dismissed him. Root next called August Hauser to the stand. August was freshly shaved and dressed in a new double-breasted cheviot suit. He deported himself with dignity and incisiveness, confirming in every detail Beaudry's version of the board meeting. The Mission Valley folk sat in choked silence as Hauser related how John Annister had accused Hilda of stealing, how the whole valley had then taken up the charge. John's clear blue eyes never left August's face; not for an instant did it occur to him that the jurymen would not see as easily as he did that the father was manufacturing his implicity in the daughter's troubles.

On cross-examination Norman asked, "Mr Hauser, Mr Beaudry testified that at the board meeting you proposed the excommunication of Mary Shoemaker?"

"Yes, I did."

"Had Mrs Shoemaker been convicted of the crime?"

"No."

"Then, isn't it true that John Annister's sole purpose at that meeting was to prevent you from punishing a woman who had not been proved guilty?"

"It was John Annister's purpose to put the blame on my daughter. That's why he said Hilda was seen coming out of the widow's house."

Root's next witness was the Widow Smithers, who was so excited she could hardly be heard above the chattering of her badly fitting teeth. Once again she had donned her yellowed wedding gown. She retold the story of the disappearance of the five ten-dollar bills from the bottom of her flour barrel after Mary Shoemaker had come in to do her baking, of the hue and cry that had been raised in the valley, of Ira Barkley's envelopes given to Hilda and Mary, and how she had gotten back the money in the mail.

"John Annister said I never had the money," the old woman cried. "But it was proved I had it because whoever took it sent it back to me."

"Mrs Smithers," said Root, "do you have in your possession the envelope in which the money was returned?"

The widow dug down into her crocheted carryall and pulled out the envelope with a triumphant gesture.

"Your honor, I ask that this envelope be introduced in evidence as Exhibit A."

Norman stepped up to the witness stand.

"Widow Smithers, isn't it true that Mary Shoemaker has been baking your bread from that same flour barrel for many years?"

"Yes."

"And it's true that she has been doing many other services for you out of pure friendship, because you have been suffering from rheumatism, and has refused to accept one cent of pay for her services even when offered it from the church fund?"

"That's so, that's so; no denying that's so."

The judge could not help smiling to himself. The courtroom did not know exactly why he was smiling, but they smiled too, feeling that something good had happened for John and Norman. At the table, Margaret relaxed from the tension that had seized her at the Beaudry and Hauser testimony.

Encouraged, Norman asked, "Isn't it also true, Widow Smithers, that upon examining the five ten-dollar bills that were returned to you in the mail, you declared before a group of your neighbors that they were not the same greenbacks that had been taken from your flour barrel?"

The widow shook her head as though unable to explain the mystery.

"They was different bills, all right."

Root waived re-examination with an offhand gesture as he summoned Hilda Hauser to the stand. She dabbed nervously at her eyes with a tiny lace handkerchief to keep back the tears. The jurors sat forward on their chairs with renewed interest.

"Miss Hauser, I know this is most painful for you,"

said Root tenderly, "but I want you to answer just one or two simple questions for me."

"Yes, Mr Root," she answered.

"Did you take an envelope addressed to the Widow Smithers from Ira Barkley?"

"I did."

"And do you still have that envelope in your possession?"

"Yes, I have it."

Her perturbation increased as she took the envelope from her purse and handed it to Root, who offered it into evidence as Exhibit B. On cross-examination Norman asked only one question.

"Miss Hauser, were you in the Widow Smithers' house on the day the money disappeared?"

Her answer was barely audible above her sobs. "Yes."

The jurors watched every move as Root sympathetically helped her down from the witness stand and escorted her back to her family. He then called on Maxwell Widney, who was dressed in his clericals, his face wan above the black cloth. His congregation sat straight on their hard benches and turned their faces up to him.

"Mr Widney, you are the minister of the Union Church of Mission Valley?"

"I am."

"You were to have been married to Hilda Hauser on June 7th?"

"Yes."

"Was the wedding ceremony performed?"

"No."

"Would you please tell the jury why not."

"It was felt necessary to postpone it."

"Why was it necessary?"

Widney looked first at Hilda, who was biting an inside corner of her mouth; then his gaze traveled slowly over his congregation, transplanted from the white church on the hilltop to this county courtroom.

". . . a minister's first duty is to his church . . . Since Miss Hauser was under suspicion . . . it was deemed wiser to clear her name first. . . ."

"Who postponed the wedding, you or Miss Hauser?"

Widney appeared wretchedly unhappy. "I did."

"Do you still love Miss Hauser?"

"Yes, I do."

"Then it was solely the implication of Miss Hauser in the disappearance of the Widow Smithers' money that caused you to postpone your wedding?"

"Yes."

"Thank you, that is all," said Root.

Norman rose slowly to his feet, his eyes and chin set hard.

"Mr Widney, you are a trained student, and you will remember accurately. Will you please tell this court precisely what happened at the board meeting in question?"

"Mr Hauser proposed that we return fifty dollars to Widow Smithers out of the church funds, and then added that Mary Shoemaker should be excommunicated as punishment for the theft. John Annister refused to allow her to be punished when she had not been convicted of a crime. Mr Hauser said that the fact that Mary Shoemaker was in the widow's house the day the money disappeared was sufficient proof to convict her, to which Mr Annister replied that Miss Hauser was also seen coming out of the widow's house that day. Mr Hauser then demanded to know if Mr Annister was charging his daughter with guilt. Mr Annister several times denied that he was doing so, to which Mr Hauser replied that since Mr Annister insisted that Mary Shoemaker did not steal the money, he was thereby accusing Miss Hauser of stealing it."

"At any time during the board meeting did John Annister accuse Hilda Hauser of stealing the widow's money?"

Widney looked out over the heads of his people. They sat watching him.

"No, he did not."

An aah-ing sigh of relief followed his words. Root came forward quickly for his re-examination.

"Mr Widney, you are devoted to John Annister, are you not?"

"Yes."

"And you are the very closest of friends."

"We are."

"You have many times gone to him for advice and guidance?"

"I have."

"Then it is safe for us to assume that you would be eager at all times to protect him and keep him from injury?"

"Yes."

"Thank you, Reverend Mr Widney. Your honor, the defense rests."

There was a moment of calm while the judge took a drink of water; Norman collected his papers and the spectators shifted their positions.

Norman's first witness was Mary Shoemaker, her loose-fitting cotton dress and scrubbed rough skin in sharp contrast to Hilda Hauser, who had buried her

False Witness

face in her arms after Maxwell Widney's testimony. In her slow-moving manner Mary testified that she had never seen any money at the bottom of the widow's flour barrel, that she had accepted an envelope from Ira Barkley only because she was forced to, and that she had burned it immediately upon reaching home.

Norman next called on John. Before taking his oath on the Bible, John took his spectacles out of their black case and hung them on the end of his nose. The jurymen hitched forward as he turned his sun-parched face toward them. Speaking slowly and simply, John related the events of the night of the board meeting, corroborating the story that Maxwell Widney had told under Norman's cross-examination. When he had finished his story, Root snapped open his glasses with a quick gesture of the wrist and advanced on him.

"My dear Mr Annister, you have lived a long time in Mission Valley; in fact, you are the founder of that community?"

"Yes."

"Before this unfortunate episode occurred, the people of your community were not given to telling tales on one another?"

"No."

"They respected one another?"

"They did."

"Before the board meeting, you never charged Miss Hauser or Mrs Shoemaker with stealing the Widow Smithers' money?"

"No."

"You had said you thought both were innocent?"

"Yes."

"Now, after the board meeting at which you talked about Miss Hauser, many people in your community talked about her?"

"Yes."

"Many accused her of stealing the money?"

"Yes."

"And that was the reason her marriage to the Reverend Mr Widney was postponed?"

"Yes."

"Then whatever you said at that meeting, whether it is remembered accurately by Mr Hauser and Mr Beaudry, or only by you, did have the effect of stirring up charges against Miss Hauser and probably destroying her prospects of marrying Mr Widney?"

John was dismayed at the trap into which Root had led him. He looked at Margaret, whose face was small and white and frightened.

"Mr Hauser stirred up the charges against his own daughter by bringing her name into the discussion and trying to make a scapegoat of an innocent woman."

"Mr Annister, since Mary Shoemaker was in the widow's house the day the money disappeared, it's humanly possible that she took it, isn't it?"

"Yes, it's humanly possible."

"That will be all."

Continuing his defense, Norman elicited from Albert Ross the information that he had seen Hilda Hauser come out of the widow's house on the day the money disappeared and had spoken of it to others; from Tim Temple, Herman Wolkskill, Burbank, Olgies and Hogarth, the confirmation that John Annister had not originated the talk about Hilda, that, in fact, he had made them promise to stop their gossiping about her.

The noon heat in the crowded courtroom was stifling; the jurors perspired in their heavy suits, growing more and more restless.

"The court will recess for an hour," announced the judge.

At the afternoon session Root apologized for taking up more time on a case which had already been established. "However, I will put on one more witness to irrefutably prove Hilda Hauser's innocence, though I regret in so doing that I must necessarily prove the guilt of another. Ira Barkley, please take the stand."

Margaret and the Martells exchanged uneasy glances, as did most of the others. Barkley was an outsider; he had no place in this trial.

"Mr Barkley, I hand you the envelope in which the Widow Smithers got back her fifty dollars. Can you identify this envelope?"

Ira patted the shoestring in his high stiff collar and arched his neck in a futile attempt to free it from its celluloid shackle.

"Yes, it's one of the envelopes I gave to Mary Shoemaker and Hilda Hauser at the board meeting."

"I now hand you a second envelope, which was entered into evidence by Miss Hauser. Can you identify it?"

"Yes, it's one of the envelopes I gave the women."

"You know that Miss Hauser testified that she did not use her envelope, and Mrs Shoemaker said she had destroyed hers?"

"Yes."

"Then, Mr Barkley, how can you be sure that these two envelopes are the ones you gave to Miss Hauser and Mrs Shoemaker at the board meeting?"

"Because in both of the envelopes I put a pinprick through the eye of George Washington."

While the spectators sat agog, the judge reached down a hand for the envelopes. He peered at the two stamps closely, ran his finger over them and then handed them to the clerk. Each juror expectantly awaited his turn to examine the first tangible evidence to be introduced in the case, to gaze at the stamps and then run his finger across them for tactile proof. Norman froze with wrath. When the last juryman had examined the envelopes, Root turned Ira Barkley over to the defense. As Norman walked past the jury box he felt a withdrawal of sympathy.

"Mr Barkley, you work for August Hauser, do you not?"

"Yes."

"Do you have any source of income other than what Mr Hauser pays you?"

"No."

"Why did you put a hole through the eye of George Washington?"

"Well, Mr Martell, I didn't know who stole the widow's money. I wanted to protect both Miss Hauser and Mrs Shoemaker."

"How were you protecting them by this secret scheme?"

169

"You see, if neither of the envelopes was used, then nobody would have the right to accuse neither of them. And if the money come back in an envelope without a hole in the stamp, then we'd all know somebody else took the money. I thought I was helping everybody."

Without anyone except Norman and Root realizing how it had happened, the focus of the trial shifted from the guilt of John Annister to the guilt of Mary Shoemaker. In his summary Root outlined to the jury his orderly presentation of the case: Mr Beaudry and Mr Hauser had established the slander; Miss Hauser had established her own innocence; the Reverend Mr Widney had shown the damage that had been done to the plaintiff. "John Annister has admitted implicating Miss Hauser in the theft; if the Reverend Mr Widney has tried to shield his friend, it is only natural for so good a man to do so. The fact has been firmly established that Miss Hauser fell into disrepute in her community only *after* Mr Annister's statement at the board meeting. As a result, Miss Hauser has lost her good name, her reputation and her prospective husband. These results more truly prove the slander than would the testimony of a thousand witnesses."

Norman was upset and heavyhearted as he once

again walked to the jury box. He recalled to the jurors the witnesses who had sworn that John Annister never accused Hilda Hauser, that, on the contrary, he had fought for her; he recalled the Reverend Maxwell Widney's categorical denial of John's guilt. He tried to make them understand that Mary Shoemaker was not on trial, that whatever they might think about her possible guilt or innocence had nothing to do with the fact that John Annister had never slandered Hilda Hauser.

Having done this, despair left him.

"Gentlemen of the jury, this is the first time the people of Mission Valley have suffered any serious trouble. Surely you can see that this case should never have been brought to trial. It should have been settled amiably among the folks at home, just as all their disputes have been settled in the four decades since John Annister opened the valley to settlement."

He paused for a moment, dramatically pointed his finger at John and bade the jury look at the defendant.

"You can see from the face and character of John Annister that he never slandered anybody. How can you convict him of destroying the peace and harmony of the community he built and loved, of injuring the happiness of any single person in that community?"

There was no demonstration, no outburst against which the judge had to bang his gavel, for the tears rolling down the cheeks of the families of Mission Valley made no audible sound.

After being instructed by the judge on the law of the case, the jury filed through a side door; the judge retired to his chambers, and talk crashed through the courtroom like a clap of thunder.

The jury remained out less than an hour. The judge entered from the opposite side of the room as they filed into their box. The people of the valley crouched forward, some of them half rising. Only John sat calmly, confident that he would not be convicted.

"Has the jury reached a verdict?" asked the judge.

"We have, your honor," replied the foreman.

"And what is that verdict?"

"We find the defendant guilty of slander and award the plaintiff five thousand dollars damages."

15

JOHN ANNISTER had enjoyed forty years of affirming by word and deed the power of good over evil; that night, as he sat on the bank watching the river spill its silver sheen across the stone ledge, he thought, "I'm too old to change my mind; too much water has flowed over this dam for me to let one injustice turn me bitter."

Margaret and her mother remained at the table under the patio oak, where the supper of bread, cheese and milk had remained untouched. During the ride home Margaret had burned white with rage at the conviction; now, as she watched her grandfather sitting alone and forlorn, the anger at last melted and she had difficulty in holding back the scalding tears she could feel pressing beneath her lids.

Coming home, a pall had hung over the train. No one had found the breath to speak, to sympathize with the Annisters.

"We'll appeal the case," Norman had said, when he had been able to conquer his unhappiness. "I'll file the papers first thing Monday morning."

John had laid a hand on Norman's knee and shaken his head slightly, his eyes veiled and withdrawn.

"No, son, we won't do that. We're through with the courts; they're no place for innocent people. I said the truth will prevail, and it will prevail . . ." That had been the last word he had said.

The sound of a rig driving up to the front gate of Mission Oaks broke the silence. After a moment August Hauser appeared along the river path. The moon was just a scimitar short of full, its clear light illumining the faces of the two men.

"John, I'm sorry for what happened," said August in a contrite voice. "It's like I told everybody in town, they didn't convict you of anything; all they did was convict Mary Shoemaker. I offer you my hand, John, and my apologies. You can understand how a father feels . . ."

False Witness

John's steel-blue eyes pierced through him. August moistened his lips; his voice grew louder.

"I've come to prove there was nothing personal in it, John. Here is the court order saying you must pay Hilda five thousand dollars . . ."

"I'll pay no five thousand dollars. I'll pay not five cents."

"Of course you won't!" cried August in his heartiest manner. "It was only Christian of you to defend Mary. Here's the order, John, and here is a release. Now we can shake hands and be friends again like I told everybody we would."

John's voice was tired and cold as he asked, "What is it you want for this paper, August?"

"I'm doing it to prove . . ."

"You want something. What is it?"

"I give you my word, John, there's nothing I want. Can't I do it for the sake of friendship? Hasn't Hilda's name been cleared? Hasn't Mary been proved guilty?"

"And now all you want me to do is declare Mary guilty."

August gave a deprecating duck with his left shoulder. "The best of us make mistakes in judgment."

John stood with his fists clenched, all sadness gone from his heart.

False Witness

"You've tried a dozen different tricks to fasten the guilt on Mary Shoe, and this trial was just another of them. August Hauser, you convicted no one in that courtroom but yourself!"

"I don't know what you're talking about," replied Hauser in cracked tones.

John's teeth set grimly. "August, well may you fear the wrath of God when He sees fit to punish you for this crime against two innocent neighbors."

The bounce and hearty confidence left August's manner; his paunch slumped; his face yellowed.

"Even after the decision of the jury, you refuse to admit Mary Shoe stole the money?"

"That jury convicted me of breaking the Ninth Commandment. I'm as innocent as Mary Shoe is of breaking the Eighth Commandment. Put that release back in your pocket, August; you'll receive not one cent of wages for your trickery."

"You'll have to pay. The law says so."

"Then I'll have nothing to do with the law."

"How long do you think you can continue to fight me?"

"I've never been a fighting man, August."

August mopped the perspiration from his brow with a colored handkerchief. Behind his bloodshot eyes

John could see him forming a decision as he automatically ran the handkerchief over his now dry and chafed forehead.

"Unless you accept the jury's verdict on Mary Shoemaker, I'll turn the judgment over to the sheriff for collection."

There was a muffled cry from the patio. Both men whirled about to see Grace Rogers come running toward them. All that day she had struggled against a foreboding of disaster.

"Don't you listen to him, Mr Hauser," she cried. "Mary Shoe stole that money just like Ira Barkley said. My father knows she stole it, and he's going to say so, same as everybody else."

She stood quivering at her own outburst, whitening her tight-clasped hands before her. John stared at her in bewilderment.

"Well, now, that's just fine, Grace," said August eagerly. "I'll turn this signed release over to you." He handed it to her with the manner of a friend presenting a gift. "As soon as your father admits Mary Shoe stole the money, you file it with the clerk of the court and everything will be all settled."

"He'll admit it," cried Grace. "He won't fly in the face of the court." To John she said furiously, "Father,

I won't let you throw away five thousand dollars. That's my money as much as yours. If Mr Hauser is so generous he'll give us a release, the least you can do is say Mary is guilty."

"My saying so wouldn't make it so, Grace."

"It was proved in court!"

"Because Ira Barkley told of a trick he played? No one in Mission Valley will believe that story."

"You'll see. Lots of people believed it."

Margaret loomed suddenly at Grace's elbow. She took the legal paper from her mother's hand with a quick firm gesture. They stood facing each other with unuttered determinations: the young girl with a passionate faith in truth and justice, in fighting for those you loved and believed in; the thick-bodied, lethargic, middle-aged woman who had been roused to action at the prospect of losing a large sum of money. All their years of bafflement and estrangement came into focus in this one instant of conflict. Seeing Margaret ranged resolutely by John's side, the two of them tempered lean and sinewy and strong, Grace perceived that they would fight on together to no matter what bitter end, that Margaret was more surely Margarita's daughter than her own. She drew a long sobbing breath, turned, walked dispiritedly through the patio and up the porch steps into the house.

Margaret quietly handed the release to August. He stood awkwardly, shrugged, put the paper into his pocket and disappeared along the river path.

16

Grace rogers' prediction about Mission Valley proved sound. After the trial several families had gone up to the clerk to ask if they might feel the pinpricks through the eye of George Washington; having acquainted their sense of touch with this tangible evidence, they had come to the conclusion that since the pinpricks were true in fact, the Barkley story must be true in essence.

"If it's enough to satisfy a jury, it's enough to satisfy us," Kearney and his wife told everyone who came into the drugstore on Saturday. "They didn't convict John of nothing," he quickly added, "but they surer 'n fate convicted Mary Shoe of taking that money."

False Witness

Those who were genuinely convinced were convinced; those who cared nothing about Mary Shoemaker and wanted the unpleasant controversy settled were convinced; those who were afraid August Hauser would move against them, as he had moved against Jerry Goucher and Henry Marden, were convinced; yet there remained a good number who made the trip to Mission Oaks to assure John they gave credence to not one word of Barkley's testimony.

The month of July should have been the most beautiful of the year, for the yucca flowers came into bloom on the Santa Monica hills and the colors of the valley deepened. The sun exploded over the Sierra Madres at four in the morning, red and hot and vital; when it set behind the western range at eight at night, the sky was awash with flaming reds and indigos, the air acridly sweet with the fragrance of fresh-cut alfalfa. Fields that had been marked with razor-thin turquoise stripes suddenly became solid green blankets of foliage; vegetables ripened and burst out of the ground; in the orchards the fruit became big and hard and bellyache green.

Yet the people of Mission Valley saw and felt no beauty. When they had learned that August threatened to turn over his judgment to the sheriff of Los

Angeles County for collection, a feeling of impending disaster stirred within them; they began to perceive that this was a death struggle in which someone would be destroyed. When they realized that Hauser had secured a list of the people who had assembled in John's dining room and was moving against them one by one, a feeling of dread seized them, blotting out the bright hot sunlight of the summer days.

James Clauves was the first to be hit. The joy of his declining years was his oldest grandson, Barton, who had graduated with honors from Glendale High School, and for whom August had secured a job in the Merchant's Bank of Los Angeles. Clauves showed up at Mission Oaks a few days after the trial, puffing furiously on his pipe.

"I was madder 'n a hornet at Jerry Goucher and Henry Marden for turning tail. But it looks like I got mad too quick."

"What's happened, James?"

Clauves jerked up his head with an angry gesture.

"Seems there be a depression in Los Angeles. The Merchant's Bank got to let a couple their newest men go." His head dropped slowly, until all John could see was the thatch of clean white hair. "I can't make Barton come back to the farm now, John, not when he's doing so good with the bank. You remember he married that Los Angeles girl . . . she always said she couldn't be no farmer's wife . . . and her expecting in a couple of months . . . It just don't seem fair to the boy to blast his life thataway."

Angus MacAdden was the next to feel the lash. A canny Scotchman, some ten years before he had suggested to his neighbors that, instead of selling their asparagus separately in Los Angeles, they pool their crops and sell it as a whole, thus commanding a better price. Because August was a smart trader they had asked him to become their representative; August had succeeded in getting as much as a cent a pound more for the asparagus than the unorganized farmers who tackled the market alone. When Angus dropped into August's office to tell him of his bumper crop and fix a date for delivery, August regretfully informed him that there had been bumper crops all over Southern California, and would Angus mind very much carting his asparagus into Los Angeles and selling it himself?

Martin Coronel had thirty acres in walnuts, a good profit crop but one that required considerable resources to gather, box and ship. For two decades Coronel had borrowed money from Hauser in July, repaying it in October. This July Hauser declared he was short on cash, that the bank in Glendale would undoubtedly help him. Coronel had thought it nice of August to suggest the Glendale bank and had driven there the same day, only to learn that they did considerable business with Mr August Hauser of San Felice and were unwilling to take over any of his permanent clients.

Four years before, when the grasshoppers had swarmed into the valley, Peter Lopez had lost his entire crop. He had been forced to borrow money from August in order to replant and carry his family. The three succeeding years had been good; Peter had not had trouble meeting his interest payments. When he drove into San Felice during the second week of July to pay his interest, he too was informed that August was hard pressed for cash, that his mortgage could not be renewed for another year. Peter would have to dig up fourteen hundred dollars or August would be forced to foreclose.

Hiram Hogarth quietly agreed that Mary Shoemaker had stolen the money; for without August's horses to shoe and August's machinery to repair, Hiram's smithy would have brought him a bare subsistence. The O'Melvanys fell in line when they heard that August was planning to import his groceries in sacks from Los Angeles. The Olgies learned that August would not be able to rent them his harvester this year; Renaldi heard a rumor that the lease on his profitable barley fields would not be renewed . . .

The fog of fear and suspicion that roofed the valley grew heavier than the summer heat haze, blotting out all clarity. The neighbor who today was stoutly declaring that Mary Shoemaker was innocent and August Hauser couldn't make him eat dirt, was the next day insisting that the jury had been right. Opinions were repeated that could have been divulged only by the closest of friends; families who were devoted on Monday were eying each other with suspicion on Tuesday, quarreling on Wednesday and not talking by Thursday.

Old differences were exhumed, ancient skeletons dragged out of closets. Three years before, Beaudry had bought a mule from Martell and the mule had gone lame that same season. Beaudry now openly accused Norman's father of palming off a crippled animal on him. Martell, ordinarily the mildest and most peaceful of souls, responded by demanding Beaudry be indicted for committing perjury against John Annister. Childless Mrs Pupke's greatest joy in life was her magnificent flower garden, which the eucalyptus windbreak, put up the year before by Atkinson to shield his seedling orange trees, killed to the last bud. After brooding over her loss for several weeks, Mrs Pupke arose from her bed at two o'clock one morning, took an ax from the barn and by dawn had cut down every one of Atkinson's eucalyptus. The Renaldis and the Bullocks had had a dispute over their west border fourteen years before, in which the Renaldis had been worsted; they now publicly charged the Bullocks with bribing the surveyor, a suspicion they had harbored silently through the years. Mrs Neill began circulating a petition to have Mary Shoemaker excommunicated from the church. Whereupon Mrs Temple, whose sister had written to tell her that she had several times seen Neill drunk in Los Angeles, started a movement to have Neill taken off the church board.

Feeling a sense of guilt at having compromised their principles to save themselves, Mission Valley experienced a need to establish guilt in others. Mrs Hamil was kept busy circulating accusations: Goucher didn't take proper care of his animals; Mrs Lopez didn't keep her kitchen clean; Mrs Beaudry crowed too much about her rich relatives; Mrs Neill nagged her husband into drinking; Herman Wolkskill made his wife bear too many children; Mrs Temple never bought a new dress; Atkinson beat his wife; Wisegane never paid his card debts . . . Private lives became public lives; scandalmongering flourished by the embroidering of fiction on basic fact; and every family in Mission Valley was quickly informed of what every other family was saying about them. Even those who had been genuinely convinced by Barkley's testimony soon found themselves embroiled. A meeting of the Tuesday coffee club broke up in a row when the members began accusing each other of spreading nasty lies, and the church social on the first Wednesday in August was a drab failure; only half the congregation appeared and, of these, few would speak to their neighbors or eat their food. Before long, quarrels broke out within families themselves; husbands argued with wives over the supper table, fathers and sons wrangled in the fields.

Mission Valley had been happy, carefree country; though the people had had to work constantly to raise their living from the soil, nature had been friendly, and they had enjoyed the company and co-operation of their fellow beings. The communal confidence upon which their lives had been based was rapidly disintegrating, not only because they could not trust their neighbors, but because they could no longer trust themselves. The open and hearty expression disappeared from the faces of the people; they began to look taut. Having established the precedent of yielding truth to convenience, having given in to force, they lived in dread of what lie they might have to tell next, what hypocrisy practice, what connivance or dishonesty perpetrate in August Hauser's war against John Annister.

By August only three families remained stalwartly with John in his determination to see justice done Mary Shoemaker: the Martells, the Wolkskills, the Temples. His friends no longer came to confess they were going over to Hauser's side or to tell him why they felt constrained to do so; he simply heard that Coronel or Lopez or Lowden or MacAdden had declared Mary Shoemaker guilty of stealing the money. And when he passed them in San Felice they averted their eyes. For John this conflict had never been a personal one; he could not feel his friends were abandoning him, only that they were abandoning fair play. He did not feel bitter about the Olgies, the Renaldis; countless times he asked himself if he had the right to demand of his neighbors that they endanger their security by fighting for an issue that did not appear to concern them directly. And yet he stood aghast at what was happening to his people and his valley.

One hot night, when there was no breath of air in the patio, John walked up the trail to the cemetery, there to sit by Margarita's grave. He felt very close to her, as though his long journey alone was nearly over. He had lived his span, he had done his work and loved his fellow men. For the first time in the thirty-six years since Margarita had left him he was glad she was not in Mission Valley to see what was happening; for the valley had been their child, Margarita's and his, and upon it they had lavished every tenderness.

After an hour of being refreshed by the cool breezes coming over the mountains from the Pacific Ocean, he stepped down the trail and stood in front of the church he had helped erect. It was too dark to see the words on the Annister plaque, but he needed no light to read them or to remember the day his mother had taken the pyrograph off the wall of her parlor and put it in his haversack.

He entered the church. It was cool and dark and clean smelling. Walking up the center aisle, he discerned Maxwell Widney sitting in the front pew with his face in his hands.

"Hello, Maxwell," he murmured.

Widney jerked up his head sharply.

"Oh . . . hello, John."

"What are you doing here this hour of the night?"

"Thinking. Or praying, maybe."

"Sometimes it's kinda hard to tell the difference."

He slipped onto the wooden bench and turned to Widney. The zest and enthusiasm were gone from the face of the young clergyman.

"I've just left the Hausers," he said. "August insists I marry Hilda before the month is up and get this affair settled."

"I always said you should marry her, son."

"I'm afraid of what device August will try next if I refuse. But it will only increase the bitterness. People will say, 'August forced the minister to do things his way too.' I'd be useless to them after that . . . What would be the sense of their coming to church to hear a hypocrite or weakling spout sermons?" He turned his earnest face to the older man. "I've had some pretty bitter scenes with August, trying to get him to stop using pressure on people. He only answers that circumstances arise in which people need his help and, if they have proved themselves to be enemies, he can see no reason to help them. I've tried to persuade him that these people have a right to their opinions, even if those opinions are against his . . ."

"August would never accept that kind of reasoning."

Widney sprang up and stood facing John with his back against the edge of the pulpit.

"Hilda has been a perfect brick. She's put our future entirely in my hands, even opposing her father on the necessity of an immediate marriage. . . . John, you're in this deeper than I am. What are we going to do about it?"

There was silence in the little church. At length John replied quietly, "Well, son, I'm going to keep on fighting in the only way left open to me: by not giving in."

Widney's fear of where and how his future father-in-law might strike next was well founded. August called a special meeting of the congregation for the following Friday night, to vote on the proposal that Mary Shoemaker's membership in the Union Church be revoked. When Norman reached the Annisters' at seven o'clock on Friday evening, he found John and Margaret already dressed and sitting in rockers on the front porch, their hands clasped in their laps, biding their time. Norman had been desperately unhappy since the trial; no amount of reassuring on Margaret's part had been able to free him from a sense of responsibility over the verdict.

When their greetings were over, Norman asked, "Gramp, do you have a copy of the church bylaws handy?"

"In the top drawer in the dining room."

Norman walked to the front door, then turned to explain.

"I want to see if they don't have to show cause before they can read a member out of the church."

"They'll say cause is she stole the widow's fifty dollars."

"An accusation isn't sufficient cause; they have to prove charges to establish cause."

"Then they'll claim the trial proved her guilty."

Norman paused irresolutely in the doorway, his eyes seeking Margaret's. She shook her head slightly, asking him to abstain. The three of them walked up to the church together.

Every family had a vote; every family was present in their regular pew, their faces uneasy in the dull light of the kerosene lamps strung along the wall. Maxwell Widney, who was sitting at a small table on the platform with Hauser and the secretary of the congregation, rose to open the meeting. As a gesture of repudiation of these proceedings, he was wearing street clothes, his low collar, dark necktie and close-fitting business suit making him appear leaner and older. He stood looking at his congregation for several moments before speaking.

"In church business such as this I have no vote. But I hope you will let me have some influence. I am speaking to you now not as your minister but as your neighbor and friend. . . . When protecting that other Mary from the fury of the mob, Christ said, 'Let him among you who is without sin cast the first stone.' By that I do not mean to infer that our Mary has committed a sin; in my heart I honestly believe her to be innocent. But even if my judgment is wrong, even if she is guilty, then I ask only those of you who have never made a mistake, never done a wrong and never committed a sin to vote against her. In that way we'll keep Mary in the church and we'll keep our church together."

He sat down abruptly. August Hauser rose, looking at Widney with fatherly indulgence.

"We are all glad our minister spoke as he did; it shows the proper Christian spirit. . . . And now we'll get on to the business of this meeting. The floor is open for discussion of the Mary Shoemaker case. The chair will recognize . . . Yes, Mrs Neill."

Sharp-featured Mrs Neill cut her way up the center aisle, then turned about and stabbed into the congregation with her righteousness.

"I say we have no right to let a thief stay in our church, any more 'n we'd let a thorn stay in our side. The Bible says, 'If thine eye offend thee, pluck it out.' Mary Shoemaker has disgraced our church. If we let her go unpunished, we set a bad example, specially for the children. They'll grow up thinking they can steal and never be punished. For the good of our families and our church we got to take away her membership."

She stopped talking and returned to her pew. No heads were turned, no eyes were shifted, but every person in the church waited for John Annister to rise from the third pew on the left and walk up to the pulpit; here, at last, the issue would be joined, the battle fought out to its conclusion. John took the black case from his vest, put on his spectacles, blinked through them for a moment, then rose and took his stand in the center aisle just under the pulpit. He looked over the heads of the congregation, through the open door that framed a section of the dark but star-studded night, and every soul there knew he was looking through their transparency to the valley beyond.

He stood without moving, without uttering a word, yet a hundred simultaneous conversations filled the little church to bursting: intimate, personal conversations that went back over the years, recalling how John Annister had welcomed them to Mission Valley, given them hospitality in his rambling Mexican farmhouse, urged them to settle there and helped find them the best land to buy and cultivate; how he had loaned them seed and tools and victuals, lumber to throw up their first rude shacks and barns; how he had helped them run in irrigation ditches from the river, widen trails into roads when they had crops to be moved; how he had loaned them money when hard times came, given comfort and council in times of adversity, sweetened their lives by his kindness. In the profound silence of the church each family relived its life in Mission Valley, feeling again the sweat on their brow as they felled the trees and broke the fields, their joy at their first harvests and the children that had come, recalling how they had worked shoulder to shoulder to build a bridge, a church, a school, a village. John Annister had been a father to them all, and in their remembering they told him clearly through the silence that they remembered. "John, remember the year the aphis got our peaches and we had to . . ." "John, remember the time my little girl took sick and you rode all night to fetch . . ." "John, remember the time I wanted to get married and I didn't have . . ." "Remember, John, remember?" And he remembered, looking through them and over them and beyond them to the valley on which he had lavished all the love that would have gone to his Margarita.

Margaret jumped up, ran down the aisle and stood by her grandfather's side, her eyes black and blazing, in her expression all the fearlessness of youth.

"You can't hound a defenseless woman out of the church; you just can't! Mary Shoe has committed no crime. How can you let her be persecuted this way? Aren't there any men among you who will stand up and denounce this meeting?"

It was the most agonizing moment the Union Church had ever suffered. But no one moved. After a moment of torturous silence John took off his spectacles, put them back in their case and returned to his pew. August rose unruffled, said, "The secretary will not include this unfortunate outburst in the minutes. Is there any further discussion? If not, we shall proceed to the vote. All those in favor of excommunicating Mary Shoemaker from the Union Church will say aye. Those opposed, nay. The secretary will please call the roll."

The secretary opened his membership book, moved the kerosene lamp a little closer and pointed the lead of the pencil to the top of the page.

"John Annister."

John's "Nay!" rang out clear and strong, and not a man or woman there but knew he was reaffirming his lifelong "Nay!" to all lies and dishonesty.

"Bill Beaudry."

Beaudry's "Aye" had a whistling sound to its intensity.

"Ralph Banning."

All eyes turned on Banning. It was several moments before he answered, then his "Aye" was so faint it could hardly be heard.

"James Clauves."

Clauves whispered "Aye" without looking up, his chin on his chest, remembering the night he had gone to John's house to vow "this time we ain't going to let August have his way."

"Martin Coronel."

Coronel looked at John supplicatingly; they had been cronies, had gone trout fishing at the headwaters of the San Felice River, had played pedro and crib-bage before a log fire on rainy afternoons when there was little work a farmer could do. He shook his head sadly as he said "Aye."

Slowly the names were called down the alphabet, slowly, sometimes inaudibly, the men replied "Aye." Only three others joined their "Nays" to John's: Temple, Martell, Wolkskill. Then there were no more names to be called; the secretary closed the book, and all that was left was for August Hauser to rise and pronounce judgment upon Mary Shoemaker.

"Come, Gramp," said Margaret firmly.

She linked her strong arm through his and helped him to his feet. Norman rose from the Martell pew behind them and took John's other arm. He walked slowly out of the church, his fading blue eyes sunk back in his head. Every family turned its face up to him as he passed, and their hearts ached, not only for what they had done this night to old John Annister, but for what they had done to themselves.

17

MARY LET HERSELF into the Annister kitchen at five o'clock Tuesday morning; by the time John and Margaret were ready for breakfast, she had the oilcloth scrubbed, the walls rinsed down with warm water, the ceiling swept with a cheesecloth-wrapped broom and hot biscuits in the oven. Grace remained locked in her bedroom. All that day Mary worked at top speed, scrubbing, dusting, washing and ironing, turning furniture upside down. She roasted a leg of lamb and, dressed in a clean calico apron, served dinner on the red-and-white-checked tablecloth in the patio. When the dishes were washed and the kitchen set in order, she joined them out of doors.

199

"You sure done us up brown today, Mary," said John.

"Yes . . . I wanted it to last you . . . a long time."

Startled by the tight quality of her voice, he took his pipe out of his mouth and asked, "Why do you say that?"

"Oh, Mr John," she cried, "I can't stay here no more. Nobody gives me work, nobody talks to me, nobody says howdy or how be you . . ."

"Well, then, you just come work for us full time. We can afford the twelve dollars a week."

"I can't do that," replied Mary, averting her eyes. "I can't work for you no more, neither."

"Why in the world not?"

"Mrs Rogers don't want me no more."

"She hasn't said so?"

"No, but don't you see how she stayed in her room all day because she don't want to look at me. She hates me for all the trouble I'm giving you. I can't stay here, Mr John. People treat me like I was dead. . . . My sister in Stockton wrote she'll take me in, providing I help with the children."

"That's just what August is trying to do, Mary, drive you out."

She sank wearily onto the very edge of the bench.

"If you could know how miserable I been since they put me out the church. I been living by myself fifteen years now, since Shoemaker got killed, but folks hereabout was kind; they let me keep their house clean, cook and sew and mend for 'em, nurse 'em when they was sick. I never did nobody no harm; all I wanted was they treat me human-like. They got no call to treat me like I was dead."

She turned away and cried silently onto the sleeve of her dress. Seeing what she was suffering, John had compassion for her.

"All right, Mary, you go live with your sister. In Stockton you'll be able to make a new life for yourself, join the church again . . . August won't give you a minute's peace until you're gone."

When she turned to him there was a touch of fire in her puffed eyes.

"It don't seem right to desert you, Mr John. I'll stay if you want me to."

"I don't want you to be unhappy; that don't help nothing."

After a moment of struggle, Mary murmured, "Before I go . . . I . . . I got a confession . . ."

"Yes?"

"I . . . I . . . well . . . I took that money! I

didn't mean to steal it . . . but when I went to bake the widow's bread that day . . . there was all that money laying in the flour barrel. . . . I needed it so bad . . . I didn't think . . ." She stopped short, gasping for breath. "Now you can tell Mr Hauser he was right, Hilda never stole that money. Then he'll stop working against you . . . and everybody in Mission Valley will be friends again . . . once I'm gone."

John sat quietly, watching her shoulders move up and down.

"All right, I'll tell August you stole the money. What shall I say you did with it?"

"Well, I . . . I . . . spent it."

"Here in the valley?"

"Yes."

"The storekeepers say you didn't."

"No, I . . . I spent it . . . in Los Angeles."

"I see. What on?"

"I needed a . . . a stove . . . a dress . . ."

"There is no new stove in your house, Mary, and you have no new dress."

She whirled about and walked to him with an air of determination.

"I sent it to my sister in Stockton!"

False Witness

"And you returned it when Ira Barkley gave you that envelope for the Widow Smithers?"

"I was sorry I took it. I wanted to make an end."

"Did you ask your sister to send the money back?"

"Yes, she sent it."

"But, Mary, you took the envelope one evening at eight o'clock, and the next morning the fifty dollars turned up at the post office. How did you get the money back from Stockton so quick?"

A bewildered expression came over her homely face.

"No, I . . . I put in the envelope . . . money I had in the house."

"Fifty dollars you had saved?"

"Yes, that's it."

"How long did it take you to save that money?"

"A long time . . . I saved . . ."

"But the greenbacks returned to the Widow Smithers were brand new."

Mary gazed at him dully, her lips moving, trying to form words. John put a gnarled hand on her shoulder.

"Mary, you make as poor a liar as you would have made a thief. You just ain't had enough practice at it."

She took his hand and held it against her cheek.

"Mr John, you always been so good to me, and all

I brought you is misery. Please, please let me tell 'em I stole the money! I'm going away . . . they can't hurt me no more . . . Then they'll let you alone. I'm ascared what they'll do to you; they'll hound you out the valley just like they done me. Please let me tell 'em I stole it . . ."

"It won't do no good, Mary, to add another lie to those already told."

It was unnecessary for Mary Shoemaker to tell Mission Valley anything; her departure was accepted gratefully as an admission of guilt. The evening after Mary left, Martin Coronel, James Clauves and the young Wisegane boy drove up to Mission Oaks in the Wisegane buckboard. Tim Temple and Herman Wolkskill soon joined them. Margaret set out on the patio table a decanter of port wine and the pound cake from Mary's last baking.

"We knew there'd be no use our coming talking to you, John," said Coronel, "seeing as how we . . . we didn't stand up for you. But we talked it over with Tim and Herman here and, seeing how they agreed with us, we all decided to come . . ."

White-haired Clauves took it up with anxiety.

"Now that Mary Shoe's gone . . . we decided to come ask you . . . to drop the whole . . ."

False Witness

"She kinda confessed her guilt by running away," chimed in the Wisegane boy.

"She didn't run away; she was driven away."

"Come now, John," retorted Coronel, "this is a free country. Nobody has to leave a place as doesn't want to."

Tim Temple had been standing back, listening to the discussion. There was an intensely serious expression on his red-cheeked face.

"John, I'll fight along with you long as you want me to," he said. "But I been thinking quite a lot these past few days: this Widow Smithers business done us all a terrible lot of harm. It can't hurt Mary Shoe none wherever she went for us to agree she stole the money."

"Ain't much use for somebody gone, fighting," declared Herman.

John looked upward into the black sky, remembering how he had lain on his army blanket that first night he had spent in this valley, watching those same stars.

"It's not Mary Shoe I been fighting for. No one person is really so important. It's what makes people what they are, keeps them human and kind and protecting each other, that's important. If we put justice and honesty aside for our convenience, what's going to protect us when we get in trouble?"

"But there's nobody else going to get in trouble," answered Coronel. "Nothing like this can happen again."

"No, it'll be something different, something we can't see now. It'll be easier to whip the second person than it was the first, because we'll be more used to it. Then a little later, maybe, it won't be just one person like Mary; maybe some family 'll be in August's way, or in whoever's way is bossing things around this valley, and you'll have to drive the whole family out because neither they nor us will have any protection left. Then one day you'll find a whole group is standing in the way of somebody's scheme or ambition, maybe all the Lutherans or Baptists that help make up our Union Church, and you'll know just how to go ahead and drive them out. Sooner or later you yourself are going to get in somebody's way, have something somebody else wants, and then you'll be the poor devil who'll be driven out. That's when you'll understand that if you hadn't sacrificed the first one, there couldn't have been a second . . . and so they could never have gotten to you. Leastways, that's how it appears to me during the days and nights when I don't do nothing much else but think about it."

There was a solemn silence while every man talked to himself. Tim was the first to speak.

"It's you we're worried about right now, John, not ourselves and the future. August will never give in until every person in the valley swears out loud Hilda be innocent. If you keep on bucking him, I'm afraid he'll try to drive you out of the valley too."

"That's exactly what I've been trying to say, Tim. If we hadn't let him drive Mary out, there'd be no fear in us now that he could drive me out."

"You're right, John, and we know you're right, every man jack of us. But knowing we're right don't do much good when we're up against a strong arm. We love you for what you're trying to do, but we're ascared for your sake. You ain't no Christ, and there ain't no need to let yourself be crucified."

It was a moment before John replied.

"There's only one fear in my heart, Martin, that something might make me give in to August's trickery. Nothing he could do to me would be as bad as that. I've lived a long time by the Ten Commandments, and I aim to continue."

The back door slammed; August Hauser came down the porch steps followed by Margaret, Grace and Mrs Hauser, who had spots of color in her cheeks. August smiled in a friendly fashion at the men awkwardly gathered around John, then went to him and put a hand on his shoulder.

"I'm glad you're not alone, John. I want everyone to hear me make my apologies to you. I've come to humble myself, to tell you you've been stronger and braver than I have. If I've seemed harsh or unjust, please remember that I had a great deal at stake. I love my wife and daughter. They've been terribly unhappy, and that's why I've done what any other father would have done in my place: fought for his family. I know how you felt at seeing Mary put out of the church, I felt bad myself, but it was a small price to pay for our harmony. Now she's gone I want us all to make up, for the sake of the valley. I'm resigning from the presidency, John, and I want you to resume as head of the church. We've all suffered a lot, and we're throwing ourselves on your mercy, to ask you to forgive us our trespasses."

There was a benign expression on his face when he finished; his voice was placatingly tender. Coronel, Clauves and Wisegane looked hopefully toward John.

"That's fair enough," put in Tim gingerly.

Mrs Hauser went to John. "Please, you promised

that night I came here . . . you would help. Be charitable . . . be kind to us like you always been to everybody. We want to see Hilda out of all this trouble and married to the minister. . . . You want that too, don't you?"

John remained motionless in his faded blue jeans, his mustache cut in a lean white line, the bones in his face standing sentinel over his sunken cheeks. There was little new he had to learn about the nature or torment of pain, yet in his aloneness and weakness he suffered now as he had not suffered since the early months after Margarita's death, his lungs barren of air, his heart empty of blood or hope. Then, as ever through the endless years, Margarita came to stand beside him, her warm hand in his, pouring faith into his empty heart and lungs, her black eyes telling him to stand firm for the right and the good.

"August, when I was a small boy in New Hampshire, I can remember our minister telling us that even the devil can quote Scripture to his own advantage. Mary Shoemaker committed no crime other than being poor and defenseless, yet you used every diabolical trick you could concoct to fasten the guilt on her, convict her in court, then drive her out of her church, her home and her community. And now you come, mealymouthing apologies, asking me to be charitable and forgiving—approve your tricks by accepting them—and as a bribe, you'll let me play at being president of our church again! It's about time you learned this, August—I tell you in front of my friends and yours, in front of my family and yours—I shall never submit to what you have done to one of our neighbors, and I shall never accept it. As long as there is a breath left in my body, I shall fight to prove that if we don't right this wrong we have done, we will destroy our valley and everyone in it."

Hauser's benignity shriveled under John's blanching fire; at last he understood there could be no amiable settlement, no convenient compromise.

"You are going to force me to collect my judgment against you?"

"You will collect nothing."

"Then I call on everyone here to bear witness that you forced me by your unreasonable and unneighborly attitude to make my next move. My attorney advises me that if you don't pay that five thousand dollars, I can have Mission Oaks auctioned off to the highest bidder!"

John's friends were thunderstruck, unable to believe they had heard aright. Sell Mission Oaks! Why, it was the first house built in Mission Valley . . . Mission Oaks had been the center of their lives . . . ! Grace's hand shot to her throat to choke back the cry that escaped half muted from between her horrified lips. She rushed to August's side and cowered before him supplicatingly.

"No, no, you can't do that! This is my home . . . you can't take my home away from me! Please, Mr Hauser, be patient, give us time; my father will admit Mary stole the money. I'll make him admit it! Mission Oaks is my property as much as his . . . it comes to me when he . . . I won't let him throw it away! Give me a few days; let me work on him!"

Margaret went to her mother's side and took her arm.

"Mother, please."

Grace shook off Margaret's hand with a frenzied gesture.

"I was born here, I tell you. I don't know no other place . . . I'd be afraid to go . . . This is my home . . . this is the only place I can live . . ."

Margaret turned to August, her slender face turned up to his, her fists knotted at her sides.

"You have succeeded in frightening my mother, Mr Hauser, but that will get you nothing. You can't bribe us, you can't frighten us, you can't force us. We will go on working for the things my grandfather has believed in all his life. You think you can bend and twist everybody to do things your way, but there is nothing you can do to make a weakling or hypocrite of my grandfather. He'll fight you and he'll defeat you!"

August cupped under his heart with his left hand, trying to hold back the pain.

"What do you say to this, John?" he demanded.

John looked at Margaret; they exchanged faint smiles.

"My granddaughter has spoken for me," he murmured.

"Then you would actually let me foreclose on Mission Oaks, let your farm and your home be taken from you?"

"Heaven's my destination, August. I'm afraid that's one home you won't be able to foreclose."

"Have you lost possession of your senses? Don't you see I can drive you out of the valley, that I will drive you out, just as I drove Mary Shoemaker out, if you don't give up this foolish struggle?"

"I'm afraid my vision is a little dimmed, August. All I can see before me is the face of Mary Shoe when she told me her old friends and neighbors treat her like she was already dead . . . and that she might just as well be dead as stay in Mission Valley."

Hauser stared at John for a moment, then turned toward the path along the river. After a few steps he stopped and walked back.

"You know by now, John Annister, I don't make idle threats. I'll give you ninety days to admit like everybody else that Mary took the money. If at the end of that time you still insist on keeping up friction and strife among our people, I'll call in the sheriff of Los Angeles County to sell your farm and drive you out of Mission Valley so you can do us no more harm."

18

THE FIRST IMPULSE, born of consternation and rage, was to rush out and stop August by sheer volume of force, cry, "You can't do this thing; this is the worst crime that could be committed in Mission Valley; this is a crime against all of us!" A few, like Jenifer up at the north pass and Olgies at the south end, actually did get into their buggies and make for town, but before they had driven far they both realized they had rendered themselves impotent: they couldn't oppose Hauser, for by so doing, they would have to admit they should have opposed him the first time, that they had behaved as cowards. They could no longer go to their neighbors to cry out in indignation and protest, plan concerted action, for the most guarded comments and attitudes were in August's possession within a few hours. Every man walked alone, afraid to speak his mind or give confidences, for it was no longer possible to know who was playing the informer, carrying tales which would bring swift reprisals. They had set out on Hauser's road and there was no turning back; they were caught in a reign of terror they had built for themselves.

Families stayed within the borders of their own farms; few people drove into the village, even on Saturdays; business came to a standstill; everyone went about his work silent and sullen. The one thing they yearned to do was to go to John Annister and tell him how outraged they were. But what good would it do to go mouthing words of sympathy when they could not say, "John, we will fight for you! We will never let August get away with this." They could not go with their hats in their hands, heads bowed, whining, "John, we're terribly sorry this is going to happen to you, but alas! we can do nothing." Better not to show one's face, not to see the heartbreak that must lie in John's eyes; better to let their old friend think they were indifferent; better anything than to let him see how powerless they were, to what weak estate they had fallen.

False Witness

Mission Oaks had been the gathering place of the valley; families had collected there when they had good news or bad, when they wanted to know how to cure an earache or hens that wouldn't lay, when they wanted to laugh or cry or swap yarns or mules. Now Mission Oaks was abandoned, and at last John Annister understood that he had become an outcast, a pariah.

He had imagined he had exhausted his capacities for bitterness, anger and despair when he had been a young man and a senseless fate had snatched from him the love that had illumined his life; now he found they had merely lain dormant these thirty-five years, that they could arise again in their full range and fury.

Though it was against his wishes, he could not help despise his neighbors for weaklings. Alternating with the bitterness was the hatred he felt, he who had never hated any man, for August Hauser. Doubts crept in unbidden, doubts about the goodness and purpose of his world if a whole lifetime of work could so easily be wiped out. In the far recesses of his mind he fought against what was, for him, the ultimate doubt: the doubt of a just God, of the God he had always loved and in Whom he had had such supreme confidence. Towering over his bitterness, his hatred, his doubt, was an overwhelming disgust: disgust with mankind, disgust with the external forms of law and justice; above all, disgust for himself because he could think of no way of stopping August, because he had permitted himself to be convicted of slander, because he had been unable to prevent Mary Shoemaker from being driven from her home, because, even now, he was powerless to keep the people of the valley from destroying both him and themselves. When he had exhausted himself with bitterness, hatred, doubt and disgust, anger washed over him like pounding breakers over a drowning man: anger with himself for thinking such unworthy thoughts and feeling such unworthy feelings. And the cycle began all over again to sap the strength from his brain and the juice from his limbs.

He no longer felt like working his farm, like going out upon the earth for a twelve-hour day of plowing, cultivating or picking. He brought in another hired man from Glendale to take over, while he spent most of his time in his bedroom, reading the Bible, or in Margarita's sitting room, sunk deep in reverie. He spoke little, even to Margaret, who was more shaken by his apparent surrender to apathy and defeat than by all the other misfortunes that had befallen them.

The quickly pyramiding events had matured her;

her girlhood was gone, and suddenly, without any apparent period of transition, she was a woman. Her face thinned, came closer to matching Margarita's delicate oval; her eyes deepened and became more resolute; even her supple figure took on an air of strength and determination. Without letting John know, she took over the management of the farm—spent hours in the fields with the men, trying to pace them, to get them to work as they always had with her grandfather, to do things his way. Despite her best efforts, she could get no response; it was not that they were lazy or indifferent, but simply that they felt nothing they might do would benefit the man for whom they were supposed to be working. At night, as she pored over the account books, she saw they were spending more money than ever before: for labor, for feed, for supplies, for repairs on equipment. Even if Hauser did not strike for several months, even if they got in their crop, it would be far below normal and would cost them money, money that must come out of John's few thousand dollars of savings.

Late one night, as John lay sleepless on his hard bed, his eyelids burning, he came to the passage in Romans: 8–28: "And we know that all things work together for good to them that love God." His eyes, reading with the swiftness of familiarity, passed on, but his mind remained with that thought. He stopped reading, took off his spectacles and murmured to himself, "We know that all things work together for good to them that love God."

In the lamplight he smiled to himself, the first smile he had known since the trial. When he rose to put his Bible on the bureau he caught a glimpse of himself in the mirror: the sunken cheeks, the fevered brow, the eyes as remote as two distant stars. That image of himself took his memory back to the other time he had looked like a death's-head, when, in his grief over the loss of his wife, he had thought only of self-destruction. Then, as now, the torrents of his bitter emotion had acted as a purge; he felt clean and new and whole again. All he was suffering was neither purposeless nor meaningless; it was part of God's plan. A calmness and strength possessed him; no matter what sacrifices were demanded, he was willing to make them when he knew that everything was working together for the ultimate good.

He went into the kitchen, made a fire and, while the tub of water was heating, prepared himself a sandwich of the roast beef that Margaret had been unable to persuade him to eat at suppertime. When the water was hot, he carried the tub into the bathroom to shave and bathe, then donned a clean nightgown, put fresh sheets on his bed and fell into an untroubled sleep.

He did not know how long he had slept, perhaps several hours, when he was awakened by the sound of a door being unlatched and footsteps coming through the kitchen and dining room. His bedroom door was thrust open; two figures appeared in the darkness.

"John, are you awake?" whispered Tim Temple in his high thin voice.

"Tim . . . what is it?"

Tim turned to the man behind him and said, "Come on in."

John sat up in bed, quickly stripping a match off the sulphur block and applying it to the wick. When the light flared he saw that Tim Temple and Maxwell Widney both had flour sacks over their shoulders.

"What in the world . . . What have you in those sacks?"

The two men slipped the sacks off their shoulders and dumped the contents onto the foot of John's bed. To his astonishment there poured out a profusion of coins and greenbacks: gleaming five- and ten-dollar gold pieces, among them big bright coins that could be nothing but twenties; dollar bills in sheafs, five- and ten-dollar greenbacks neatly folded into packages; twenty-dollar bills yellow on one side and green on the other; fifty-dollar notes as clean as though they had been printed an hour before; highly polished silver cartwheels, half dollars blackened with usage, a shower of quarters, dimes, nickels and dull bronze pennies. They fell in a great heap on John's blanket, making a pool of gold and silver and paper green in the lamplight.

"Where does this money come from?" he exclaimed.

"From Mission Valley," replied Widney with a grim smile.

"It was Maxwell's idea," cried Tim. "Everybody here wanted to help you, but nobody knew how. So Maxwell said, everybody take part of the responsibility, everybody contribute what he can. We told the whole valley—excepting August, Beaudry, Mrs Neill and Mrs Hamil—then Ralph Banning put a big washbasket under his rear counter. We ain't got the faintest notion where the money come from, John, or how it got there, but here it be, five thousand dollars' worth! It come out of old trunks and old socks and old drawers and tin cans and holes in the ground and penny banks and big banks."

False Witness

John sat up in bed, looking at the money with tears in his eyes. Widney spoke to him gently.

"Everybody put in everything they had, John, to show how much they love you and believe in you."

"We counted the money tonight, back of Marden's," continued Tim. "You know, where he keeps that printing press of his? There was a little over thirty-seven hundred dollars the families put in that basket. Banning, Marden, Hogarth, O'Melvany, Kearney, Herman, me and Maxwell made up the balance. It's all here, John—five thousand dollars, right down to the last Abe Lincoln penny."

John got out of bed and put a hand on Maxwell's shoulder, shaking his head at him with a sad smile.

"It was a fine and loving thought, Maxwell . . . but I can't accept the money."

"You don't have to," laughed Tim. "Here it is . . . it's yours . . . it don't belong to nobody else."

"If I paid five thousand dollars to August, I'd be proving to people how profitable it is to trick your neighbors. Look, Tim, Maxwell: we don't dast reward Hauser for what he's done!"

"It would be a kindness on your part," replied Widney, "if you would let the people of the valley pay their debt to you in this way; they'll feel they did their little bit in settling things satisfactorily. It 'll make it possible for them to live with themselves again."

John stood up straight and stern.

"They're trying to get off cheap, Maxwell. They can't meet their obligations by secretly throwing money into a washbasket."

"It's the only way they have," ventured Tim.

"That's where you're wrong. They still got hind legs to stand up on and be men. They can still come out in the broad daylight and fight for what they know to be right."

"But we can't return this money," protested Tim. "We don't even know who put in how much."

"Just dump it back into the basket under Banning's rear counter and tell folks to come take out as much as they put in."

Grace slipped into the room, her hair in paper curlers, her bathrobe held tightly around her.

"Don't let him give this money back," she pleaded. "The people gave it to us and it's ours! Isn't it, Tim? Isn't it, Reverend Widney? Carry it over to the Hausers tonight . . . throw the sacks on his front porch. Then we'll be through with all our worries."

Margaret restrained her mother from scooping the money into the sacks.

"Please, Mother, you mustn't go against Gramp. Can't you see he's right? Can't you see we have to do things his way?"

"No, I can't," cried Grace. "I think he's going out his mind! I'll go to court, I tell you! I'll have him declared—yes, I will—crazy!"

There was a flat, horrified silence in the room.

"For shame," said Margaret in a tone that left little else to be said.

Grace whirled about, her face contorted, her arms raised as though she were going to strike her daughter.

"It's not right you should side against your mother! It's not natural for a daughter . . . You never did love me . . . now you're proving it . . . my own flesh and blood fighting me . . . getting me put out of my own home. A daughter should help her mother, and listen to her, and spend her time with her, and take care of her and make her happy. But you never liked to be with me . . . your own mother . . . who brought you into the world . . ."

She burst into a flood of tears, masking her pudgy face with pudgy fingers. Margaret stood above her mother, her face pale and drawn. After a moment she led the weeping woman from the room.

"John, I didn't want to tell you," said Widney.

"The reason I tried this idea . . . August is going ahead with his plan to sell Mission Oaks on his judgment."

"Yes, I know."

"But we've got to stop him!" exclaimed the clergyman.

"No," replied John, "I won't stop him."

"You'd let him take Mission Oaks?" cried Tim, aghast.

"Tim, I didn't start this affair. I never had anything to do with it, excepting to try to protect Mary Shoe. I have no intentions of bargaining with the devil."

"But, John," protested Tim, "he'll do to you what he did to Mary Shoe . . . he'll drive you out the valley . . ."

"Maybe it's necessary I let August drive me out the valley. Maybe by letting people see the full results of what they've done, they'll come to understand you can't compromise with truth."

"My year is nearly up," said Widney in a lethargic voice. "I'm going to resign. If I stay here and watch August do this to you, it will kill everything I've found . . . in the church . . . in religion. I've got to go away . . . if for no other reason than to save myself. . . . When I'm established somewhere, I'll send for Hilda."

False Witness

For a moment nothing could be heard but the sputtering of the wick.

"Son, this may be the last time I will be able to tell you this: but stay! We've been an innocent people, protected from the outside world by our mountains. There's a new age outside our valley, a new century that preaches dog eat dog, and every man for himself. If I give in to August now, that new age will begin in our valley. We have to show the folks they must fight, even with their homes and their lives, to protect the things they've grown up with: their freedom, their friendship. I want you to be here to show them what it all means, Maxwell; they're going to need guidance when they see the trap they've led themselves into. You'll be the only one they'll listen to or believe, for you'll be the only one who made no compromise. God has given you this vineyard to plow, my boy, just as He gave it to me nearly forty years ago. I'm going to finish out my work here the way I think it should be finished, and you must do the same."

19

SEPTEMBER CAME; the fruit ripened on the trees, the grain in the fields. Every fall there had been husking bees, barbecues and barn dances to celebrate the reaping; this year the Tuesday coffee club was no longer meeting; only six families had attended the church social on the first Wednesday. The Clauves, Jenifers, Olgies, Libbets and Trainors drove into Glendale on Sunday mornings to attend the Methodist church; the Burbanks, Gouchers, Kearneys, Lankershims, Hubbards and Keyes decided to ask the next Baptist Convention to send them a circuit preacher once a month; the Martells, Temples, Wolkskills and many others stayed away from church entirely.

Early rains slashed through the north pass; the fields

were concealed under a violet haze and the houses sat like whitecaps on the storm-tossed earth. Some little carpentry could be attended to in the barn, leather harnesses and other gear could be patched; in the tool-shed the tools could be oiled and sharpened; but when these things were done everything was done; there was nothing left to do but wait for the storms to pass. While the people sat indoors they brooded over what had happened to them and their valley, made heroic resolutions; but it was raining out, so they just rocked and hoped for the best.

On the first of November, notices were posted at strategic points in the valley, stating that Mission Oaks, with its forty acres of farmland, house, barn, sheds, stock and equipment would be auctioned off to the highest bidder on Saturday morning, November 14, 1903. It took this physical sight of the posters to convince the valley that the sale of Mission Oaks was no ghastly, incredible dream, like reading one's own death notice in the paper.

With the passage of the days Norman had shown John how he could stave off the auction for another nine months; the Martells had begged him not to dispossess himself of the home he loved; the Temples and Wolkskills had pleaded with tears in their eyes that he do something, anything, to keep Hauser from crushing him; Renaldi, Hogarth and Lopez had urged him to give in to Hauser for the moment, pledging themselves to fight later, when circumstances were more favorable; August came once again to request that John utter the three small words, "Mary is guilty"; Grace wept and stormed, pleaded and cursed. But John stood firm; he was determined to prove that right was right and that truth would prevail.

The day of the auction dawned clear and cold. By seven o'clock the first buggies had come up the road and parked in front of the wall John had built of field stones. By eight o'clock the roadway was choked with wagons, buggies, rigs, the lawn covered with bicycles. By nine-thirty everyone in the valley had assembled: the aged, the sick, the weak, the lame, the infants still nursing at their mother's breast; only Hilda Hauser was missing, August having sent her to visit with an aunt in Los Angeles. A high wind whipped across the fields, coating the edges of the floating clouds with a layer of dust, and the folk of Mission Valley stood under the great Annister oak, waiting for a miracle. In its place came August Hauser with a deputy sheriff.

At ten o'clock John emerged from the house wearing his faded blue overalls and workshirt, carefully shaved, his gray and black hair combed back flat against the lean head, his mustache clipped, his spectacles sitting on his nose. He stood above the steps of his porch, looking as indigenous and unprootable as the oak under which he had slept during his first night in this valley. Margaret took her place beside him, her arm linked through his.

The sheriff's deputy, in an enormous sombrero hat and wide leather belt which he had trouble in buckling around his portly middle, mounted the steps of the Annister house. All faces turned to him, faces somber and silent.

"Mr Annister, I have here a court order to auction off your farm to the highest bidder. If you are willing to pay the five-thousand-dollar judgment, the sale will be called off."

John's eyes roamed over the Santa Monica hills, stopping where a few white crosses were visible on the knoll above the church.

"Have you anything to say, Mr Annister, before I proceed with this auction?"

After a painful pause the sheriff drew an official paper from his pocket and began to read in a monotone: " 'Pursuant to a writ of execution issued by the Supreme Court of the State of California, in and for the County of Los Angeles, it is hereby declared that the property of John Annister, herein known as Mission Oaks, is to be sold to the highest bidder.' The auction is now open. What am I bid for this forty acres of land, house, barn, sheds, stock and equipment?"

Half his words were blown away, but there was no need for the people assembled in the Annister yard to hear them. Those of his friends who had planned to bid and buy back Mission Oaks for him had been forbidden by John to do so; those few who would have liked to steal the property at a ridiculous price were afraid to anger Hauser by bidding at all. Only the wind spoke, in deep terms of displeasure.

"I ask for the second time, what am I bid for this forty acres of land, house, barn, sheds, stock and equipment?"

Again the sheriff looked at the crowd; the crowd looked at John; John turned his face to Margaret, one corner of his mouth lifted in a wistful smile.

"For the third and last time, what am I bid?"

"I bid five thousand dollars," said August Hauser.

For an instant even the air was still; in the acute silence everyone heard what everyone else was feeling and thinking.

False Witness

"I am bid five thousand dollars. Are there any other bids? Who will give more?"

No one moved. Margaret tightened her hold on John's arm. The sheriff repeated his demands for further offers, then said, "Are you all done? Going . . . going . . . gone! Sold to Mr August Hauser for five thousand dollars."

John turned and went into the house. Bewildered, sick of soul, the families shuffled with averted eyes to their wagons and drove away. Soon the yard was abandoned, and quiet fell over Mission Oaks, a quiet lashed by the powerful sweep of the wind.

That night, while John roamed about Margarita's sitting room, striking a lonely haphazard note on the piano, and Margaret sat numb and impassive at the dining-room table under the light of the green lamp, Norman came through the kitchen and stood before her, gasping for breath, his hands bleeding, his trousers torn, his face caked with sweat. She rose quickly, took him in her arms and ran her finger tips down his cheek.

"Norman, what is it?"

A tremor shook him; then he stepped back and handed her the piece of rough-hewn wood he had been clutching. She gazed at it uncomprehendingly, murmured, "Thou Shalt Not Bear False Witness against Thy Neighbor." Her eyes shot up to his suddenly. "Why, Norm, that's Gramp's plaque from the church . . . !"

She stood rigid, staring at him, her eyes leaping to fire, her lips quivering. "Norm, what does it mean . . . ?"

When he could only stand before her, his face blanched with rage and compassion, Margaret knew that John Annister had been excommunicated from the church he had founded. All the misery of the past months, all the bitterness of that morning hour when the Annisters had been humiliated before their own people, burst forth in heartbroken sobs. Norman knew there could be no words of comfort; he could only hold her tight and strong against him.

"August thinks he has to drive Gramp out of the valley to keep Hilda's name clear. He called a meeting tonight at his home. My family wasn't told, neither were the Temples or Wolkskills, because they've been staying away from church, or the Olgies, Libbets, Clauves, Jenifers or Trainors, because they've been going to Glendale to services; he sent no word to the Kearneys, Hubbards, Burbanks, Keyes, Gouchers or Lankershims on the grounds that they had deserted and forfeited their votes. Even Maxwell Widney didn't know of the meeting."

Margaret sank onto a chair and sat looking up at him, holding one of his hands.

"He had the whole thing arranged beforehand . . . made a speech telling how a fair and impartial court had convicted John of slander . . . Since he had violated one of the Ten Commandments, he had to be put out of the church. When he asked for a vote, there wasn't a person dared stand up against him. I . . . I tried, Margaret. I made them listen to me . . . I lashed August Hauser with every crime he had committed: against Mary Shoe, against Gramp, against the valley. But I couldn't move them; they just sat there. Then he had another resolution passed to cut the Annister plaque out of the front beam . . . so the valley could forget John and all the trouble he caused them. I couldn't let any of them put their hands on that plaque . . . so I ran up to the church myself . . ."

Margaret made no attempt to stem her tears.

"Poor Gramp," she whispered, "all these years he's waited to join his Margarita on that hill. It's the cruelest blow of all, Norman, to keep him from her."

John spoke from behind them in the dark doorway of the sitting room.

234

False Witness

"They can't keep me from my Margarita." He came to the young couple, raised Margaret from her chair, put an arm about each of them. "They won't let me stay in their church; they won't even let me be buried in their cemetery beside my wife. But time will vindicate me, time and you two children. And then I'll come back to that knoll where I first crossed over from the ocean and found my home place. Eternity is a long while; surely I can wait for it a little longer?"

False Wines

} 20 {

EARLY MONDAY MORNING Margaret and Grace rode into Los Angeles with Norman to look for a house. By mid-afternoon they had found a bungalow on Alvarado Street with a moss-covered well in the front yard and a stretch of flower garden at the back. After she had paid a month's rent, Margaret caught the train for Glendale, then drove the mare through the valley into the deepening sunset. This was the last time she would ride along the familiar road in the cool, color-splashed dusk; with all the fierce pride of the Abilas she resented being driven from her home; with the gentleness of the Annisters she ached at the thought of leaving the valley in which she had been born. Sitting up straight and stiff in the buggy, her head held high and her fragile face set into the wind, her bosom hard against adversity, she made her vows: she would never rest until the Annister name was vindicated, until Annister hands and Annister sweat once again farmed Mission Oaks.

In the morning the Martells, Tim Temple and his buxom Stella, Herman Wolkskill and four of his strapping sons came to Mission Oaks to load its furniture into the Martell and Annister wagons. The contents of Margarita's sitting room were carefully wrapped and sent to the Martell house to be guarded against the day when they could be brought back to the room in which they belonged. Tiny Tim worked like a madman, carrying out pieces of furniture three times his size to conceal his feelings, but Herman could only sit limply on the front step and blow his nose too loudly into a red bandanna handkerchief. Stella, Mrs Martell and Margaret helped each other in the kitchen, packing glasses and dishware into barrels. John remained in his bedroom, reading the Bible, hardly aware of the activity going on about him. At length the moment arrived when Tim and the oldest Wolkskill boy had to knock at his door and tell him the time had come.

Margaret took the reins of the Annister wagon,

with John at her side. The valley was deserted as they drove through: no farmer could be seen in his fields, no housewife in her yard; none had come to say good-by. She guided the horses with her face set stonily ahead, but John surveyed the orchards and furrows. After a time they reached the south pass, into which John Annister had ridden with his farm wagon, his household goods and his bride almost forty years before. At the last moment he turned on the high seat to look back at the valley, and Margaret sensed that it was a farewell, that the eyes that had watched its transformation from a wilderness never again expected to gaze upon Mission Valley.

The bungalow on Alvarado Street was small but comfortable. The Annister furniture, curtains and knickknacks spread about the house gave them a feeling of being not altogether in a foreign land. John's bed, bureau and night table were set up in the front bedroom overlooking the moss-covered well. He hardly seemed to notice the transition, spending the better part of the day in his room reading Scripture, or lying stretched out on his bed with his hands locked behind his head, gazing up at the portrait of Margarita and retreating into the past. Sometimes, of an afternoon, Margaret was able to persuade him to go into the back garden and sit for an hour in the sun, but she soon learned that he was acquiescing to please her. He ate little, and she knew he rarely closed his eyes, for she heard him moving about his room at all hours of the night. With each passing week he appeared to age a year: the skin stretched taut over the bones of his face, his head shrunk in size, his walk slowed, his shoulders became stooped, his gaze uncertain.

Norman came every evening to the Annister cottage. Sometimes, when John had sat through supper with his chin on his chest, not touching a bite of food, Margaret would ask Norman to take her out for an hour. They walked to the little Alvarado park, with its magnolias and palm trees, and sat on a bench in the cold moonlight so that she could bury her face on his shoulder for the cry she would not permit herself at home.

"Norm, can you see how he's failing . . . day by day . . . He's dying under our eyes . . . and we can't do anything to stop it."

"I'm afraid he wants to die, Margaret."

She lifted her head, the tears making her eyes soft and luminous. "I've tried to go out and work for him . . . to check back on the witnesses . . . to get new evidence . . . but he won't let me do anything. He just pats my hand . . . tells me to wait, the time will come . . ."

The days of winter passed slowly. There was a good deal of hard, pelting rain. Only once did John bestir himself, in late February, asking Norman to send him a buggy and driving off by himself. He returned in the afternoon, more at peace than he had been since the rains began. He went out of doors a little after that, rigging up an old wooden bucket over the well, filling it and listening to the drops tinkle into the water below.

With spring, the flowers in their back yard broke through the crust of earth from the seed dropped in the fall; the grass in Alvarado park became a brilliant green carpet. All about him, nature was renewing itself in the miracle of rebirth that had always brought John Annister fresh vigor. But this spring there were no fields to be planted; there was no rebirth. One night Margaret heard him coughing in his room; in the morning, when she took in his breakfast tray, she found him feverish. She summoned a neighborhood doctor, who reported a temperature of a hundred and three, a weakening pulse.

Margaret sat by his bedside all day. He opened his eyes to look at her once or twice, but never spoke. At sundown he asked to see Grace. Margaret summoned her mother. She heard the low murmur of John's voice, Grace's bitter weeping. When Grace had left her father's room and Margaret re-entered, he whispered: "I'll rest now. When Norman comes . . . I want to see . . . you two . . ."

Norman arrived from his office at six. Margaret led him into John's room. They stood above him, gazing down at the bone-rutted face, the yellowed mustache. After a moment he opened his eyes. Margaret sat on the edge of the bed and took his hand in hers.

"I wanted to tell you children. When I'm gone . . . you will be free to work. . . . You will prove August tricked us. . . . Mission Oaks will come back to you. Norman, in the top drawer . . . my bureau, the paper . . ."

Norman opened the bureau drawer, took out a paper and handed it to John.

"It's my will . . . That's where I went in the buggy . . . Margaret, I left you Mission Oaks . . . Live there with Norman . . . have lots of children . . . teach them to love the valley . . ."

"I will, Gramp, just as you taught me."

"Teach them to be good . . . not to hurt other people . . ."

"I promise, Gramp dear."

John looked up at Norman.

"Son, take care of her . . . help her get back Mission Oaks . . ."

"I will, Gramp."

John returned his smile, then closed his eyes. All night they sat by his bed, watching. Just before dawn he moved slightly, turned his eyes to the picture of Margarita looking down at him, and sighed deeply.

The Martells, Temples and Wolkskills came in the next day for the funeral. No one wept as they stood about the grave in the bright spring sunlight, not even Margaret. No services were held, no prayers uttered, no words spoken. They would all have to be patient; there was work yet to be done before they could put John Annister to rest.

21

ON FRIDAY Margaret returned with Norman to Mission Valley. It was the first time she had gone back since the day she had driven through the south pass with her grandfather; as she rode homeward in the Martell buggy, she thought how empty the valley would feel without him to wave her a welcome from his rough chair under the oak.

Mrs Martell had prepared a chicken dinner, inviting the Temples and Wolkskills; they told tales of the time John had been boosted over the Hubbard fence by a new bull, the night he had thought his barn was on fire and had rushed in with two buckets of water, only to find the Wolkskill boys in the haystack, trying to learn how to smoke.

243

False Witness

Later Margaret and Norman walked over to Mission Oaks. The plants around the house had their spring bloom of flowers and berries, and the lawn was well tended, the work of Tim Temple. Margaret stood in silence before the dark empty house.

"Let's go sit by the dam," suggested Norman. "It'll be nice there."

They sat on the bank, watching the spring freshets spill over the stone ledge. The night-blooming jasmine filled the air with a heavy sweet scent.

"Norm, I'm starting work tomorrow, here in the valley."

"Mother wants you to make your home with us until . . . until we can move into Mission Oaks."

Her eyes expressed her gratitude. Then she said, "Now you must tell me what we have to do."

"We have to file a bill of complaint against the Hausers to set aside the sheriff's sale, on the ground that fraud has been perpetrated and that the facts have only just been discovered."

"Then it's up to us to find new facts." Her agitation made her spring to her feet. "Norm, I'll find that new evidence. I'll begin tomorrow on Ira Barkley."

Norman remained seated, winding an index finger through his curly brown hair as he thought.

"Barkley is the keyman, all right."

Ira Barkley was not at all pleased to see her. He perched perilously on the edge of a rocker in the Neill parlor, looking gaunter and yellower than ever before.

"I'm a sick man," he whimpered, sliding an index finger inside the high celluloid collar to ease the red line across the cords of his neck.

"Please, Ira, go back to the beginning. There must be something . . . When you reached your office the morning the letter came with the fifty dollars in it . . ."

"I won't be cross-examined," he broke in.

"I'm not going to cross-examine you," she replied softly. "I only want you to help my grandfather."

"But I can't help nobody, and that's the end of it."

"It's by no means the end of it, Ira; it's only the beginning."

Barkley wiped a crumpled handkerchief across his lips. "I don't know nothing . . . I told what I know . . . I don't know nothing more. . . ."

Unrelenting, Margaret worked on him for three hours, questioning, probing, dissecting; she could not get him to go back on the story he had told in court. When the grandfather clock in the Neill hall tolled eleven, she saw a greenish flush spread over Barkley's face; his hand shot to his throat to throttle the rising nausea. He sprang up from his rocker and fled without a word, leaving Margaret feeling guilty and frustrated.

The next morning Norman drove her across the valley into an elongated, razor-sharp strip of ground haze that hugged the base of the mountains like a white bandage, leaving the upper ranges revealed in stark sunlit clarity. The Albert Ross farm seemed more dilapidated than ever. Albert had consistently bad luck with his equipment; each passing season saw more of it piled in a discarded heap in the front yard. They found him astride a crossbeam in his barn, repairing a hole in the roof in a spirit of hopeful futility.

"Will you come down, please, Albert," Margaret called up to him.

"Would it be a botheration to come back another time?" asked Albert. "Looks like it's fixin' to rain tonight, and I ain't had a chance to patch up this hole yet."

"We want to talk to you," said Norman in a tone that left no leverage for argument.

Albert accidentally kicked over his ladder, then had to hang from the beam by his hands and land in the hay. He made a long task of righting the ladder, palming the perspiration from his forehead up into his hair.

False Witness

"Albert," said Margaret, "if you hadn't gossiped about seeing Hilda come out of the widow's house, the fifty dollars would have been forgotten overnight . . ."

"I seen Hilda come outen the house, and I said so. The Constitution says a man's got a right to talk!"

"Yes. That's precisely what you're going to do now: talk! At what time did you see Hilda Hauser leave the widow's house?"

Albert rolled a cigarette so bumpy the thin brown paper burst over the center of the tobacco, then rolled a second one with a solemn, thoughtful air.

"August Hauser 'll boot me off 'n this farm if I open my face."

"Don't be a coward!" Margaret exploded.

He stood with his head down, his knees sagging, puffing on the saliva-wet cigarette. He spoke without lifting his eyes to theirs.

" 'Tain't much of a farm, but it's the only farm I got."

He climbed slowly up his ladder and stood blindly hammering on the board patch. Norman took Margaret's arm and led her from the dark, manure-smelling shed.

When Norman returned to his office on Monday,

she settled down to a concentrated regime. She spent the morning in the fields with Bill Beaudry, trudging by his side doggedly as he plowed under the wild mustard, matching her determination against his sullen silence, reasoning with him, pleading, flinging her passionate anger into his teeth, flinting herself against his indifference, his stolidity, his harsh words and clumsily veiled insults, using every strategy to make him agree that he had been mistaken in his testimony.

"I didn't commit no perjury, and don't you go round saying I did! I told things just like I remembered them."

"Bill Beaudry, your father loved John Annister and called him his best friend. Have you no sense of family loyalty? Why don't you stand by your father's friends the way he would if he were alive!"

Beaudry flung his plow over on its side with a rough gesture of denunciation, confronting her with blazing eyes.

"I don't let no man talk to me like that. No, and no woman, neither. You don't belong in this valley any more, Margaret Annister. Get off my property and leave me be."

That evening she spent alone with the Widow

Smithers in her vine-covered cottage; though the widow had always seemed ageless, Margaret saw that she had grown years older in the passing months. She was now deserted and disconsolate, no longer enjoying the excitement and mystery of the drama she had promulgated, for her few remaining pleasures in life were gone: the friendly Sunday morning gatherings in the white church on the hill, the Wednesday night socials, the sewing circles, the shopping crowds in San Felice on Saturdays, the neighbors who dropped into her house to chat, the feeling of being part of a prosperous, comradely, up-and-coming community, all were gone.

"It isn't too late yet, Widow Smithers," Margaret told her. "You can still save my grandfather's name, and Mission Oaks, and the peace of our valley. If you never had that fifty dollars, please, please tell the truth now."

The widow itched her gums against each other with a sideward movement, then answered in a hoarse voice, "I positive had the money. I wish I never found it in Smithers' trunk . . . but I positive did."

The next day she drove the Martell rig to the bank in Glendale. The cashier, a plump little man with a moonface, was an old friend of the Annister family.

He welcomed Margaret into his dark mahogany-paneled room and sat her next to him before the enormous desk.

"I was mighty sad to hear about your grandpa passing on. Fact to tell, we've all been mighty regretful about this Widow Smithers business. I hear the Jenifers and the Clauves are offering their land for sale. That's a bad sign; it'll hurt property in the valley . . ."

"Then perhaps you'll do something for me?"

"Anything, Miss Margaret, anything I can."

She spread her hands on the hard flat desk before speaking.

"Search the bank records . . . See if August Hauser withdrew fifty dollars shortly before the widow got her money back in the mail . . ."

The cashier shook his head with a wistful smile.

"That would be against bank rules. We're not allowed to divulge our clients' affairs."

"But if I can prove that Mr Hauser drew five ten-dollar bills from the bank just before . . ."

The cashier rose and stood bouncing up and down on the balls of his toes.

"Speaking as your friend and not the cashier of the Glendale Bank—why don't you go to Mr Hauser's office and demand to see his check stubs? Surely, if he had nothing to conceal . . . ? It would be a most logical procedure for you to think of yourself. . . ."

Before returning to San Felice, she waited for the noon arrival of the lone train operating between Los Angeles and Glendale. The conductor remembered that Hilda had acted "excited-like" the day after the widow's money had disappeared, but he had attributed that to the buying of a new dress. Back in San Felice, she drove directly to the Hauser office, studying August's bulky back for a moment before she entered. They stood appraising each other in silence; neither mentioned the death of John Annister.

"Mr Hauser, I came here to ask you to let me examine your check stubs for the week preceding the return of the Widow Smithers' money."

August's face darkened to the peculiar rose-purplish hue that preceded his heart attacks.

"You have your nerve about you! My checkbooks are my private affair. I allow no one to meddle in them."

"I'm not trying to meddle; all I'm trying to do is locate a certain withdrawal check . . . for fifty dollars. If you have no such withdrawal in your books, you won't be afraid to let me examine them."

"You're barking up the wrong tree, young woman," shouted August. "I'm a very busy man. Good day to you!"

Margaret drove as fast as she could to the Hauser home, toying absently with the accumulated bric-a-brac on the mantelpiece until Mrs Hauser came through the painted acorn screen that separated the parlor from the dining room. Margaret started toward her impulsively, speaking as she walked.

"I've just come from your husband's office . . . He refused to let me examine his check stubs. You've got to help me . . . You've got to persuade him."

Mrs Hauser stood pale and frightened-eyed before the outburst, clutching the strings of acorns to support herself.

"Make him . . . show his check stubs? But I can't . . . I have no influence . . ."

"Then take the stubs from his office! I'll tell you the exact dates I want. You owe that much to John Annister. He tried to help you when you were in trouble . . . when you came to him crying . . . to protect Hilda's name . . ."

The very thought of taking anything from August's office made Mrs Hauser shake with nervous spasms. She tried to speak but could make no coherent reply. Margaret helped her to the blue plush sofa.

"I'm sorry, Mrs Hauser," she said, contrite. "It was wrong of me to upset you so. But there is one thing you can do for me . . . Give me the address of the aunt Hilda is staying with. I have never been able to . . . talk to Hilda . . . but I'm going to try now. I don't think she fully understands . . ."

Mrs Hauser looked up with faded, beaten eyes and murmured, "I can't . . . I can't even give you Hilda's address."

"But why not?"

"August has forbidden me . . . If I went against his wishes . . . Oh, please, please, we're all so desperately unhappy. Couldn't you just bear your part of the burden . . . and let us bear ours?"

Out of pity, Margaret forbore. The horse picked his own way home to the Martells', while she sat crumpled on the bumpy leather seat.

A night's sleep refreshed her. The next morning she was at Banning's when he opened the store at seven o'clock. Banning's condolences on the death of her grandfather were genuine, but he would not yield to her entreaties to commit himself on what had happened that night at the board meeting.

"A storekeeper mustn't take sides," he kept repeating.

"Mr Banning," she cried in exasperation, "you've

been saying that exact same sentence in that exact same tone for twenty-five years!"

"That's right, Margaret, and it's kept me out of a heap of trouble."

"But there are times to stay out of trouble and times when we should jump into it with both feet!"

"No, Margaret, trouble is a thing a man ought to stay out of always, especially a storekeeper."

From Banning's she went to see Neill, who had been drinking more steadily than ever. Neill led her behind the barn, out of sight of his wife's surveillant window, then got a load off his chest.

"I been wanting to tell 'em right along, only my old lady wouldn't let me . . . Hauser and Beaudry both fibricated at that trial! John didn't accuse Hilda of nothing . . . I was at that meeting, cold sober too, so I ought to know. Poor old John was only trying to defend Mary Shoe. . . ."

Margaret wrote down every word in her stenographer's notebook. When he had finished his outburst, she handed him the notebook and pencil.

"Will you sign this for me, Neill? It'll be valuable to me when we go into court again."

Neill peered about cautiously, rescued a jug of whisky from its cache in a near-by pepper tree, took a long swig and then, reinforced, pulled out the sheet of paper on which Margaret had been writing and tore it into bits.

"I can't sign no paper," he proffered apologetically. "My wife 'd kill me."

Each night, before she went to sleep, Margaret wrote down a summary of what had occurred during the day: the interviews, the admissions, the denials, the evasions, the truths that had somehow emerged. Each morning she outlined her program: the people she would see, the leads she would follow, the material she would try to uncover. She visited every family in the valley in turn: the Burbanks, Gouchers, Olgies, Clauves, Jenifers, Celises, Mardens, Hogarths, Renaldis, Kearneys, Bullocks, Libbets, Keyes, Lankershims, O'Melvanys, Lopezes, Wiseganes, Sepulvedas, asking for help, for information, for ideas. She went to Mrs Hamil, who knew everything that had been said and thought in Mission Valley; Mrs Hamil emitted a jet of words that lasted for several hours but brought Margaret nothing. Several times she went to see Maxwell Widney, who helped her analyze her problem and get off to a fresh start.

When Norman returned home on Friday night, she told him everything she had done, showing him her written reports. Norman did not find them encouraging.

"Then I'll have to begin all over again," she said. "There must be a weak link somewhere. When we find it, we'll break through to the truth."

She began her tireless rounds again. This time she was able to fret Ira Barkley into two contradictions; this time she was able to elicit from Albert Ross the information that he had wondered why Hilda Hauser had waved to him so gaily the day he had seen her coming down the widow's steps, "uppity Hilda, who treated me like I was dirt under her feet." This time she led the Widow Smithers into revealing that Hilda "always had her hands and nose in everything when she come avisiting"; this time she was able to make Banning admit that "August had come to the board meeting determined to fasten the guilt on Mary Shoe, no matter what the cost." But she knew even before Norman told her that she had unearthed no new evidence of any value.

The one week for which she had come to Mission Valley lengthened to an entire summer. She worked from early morning to late at night, racking her brain for new approaches, going back again and again to people who had grown tired of her troubles, who were frightened at the possible consequences of her efforts, who barred their doors and their hearts against her in their desire to be left alone, who began to blame her and her grandfather for the breakdown of business in San Felice and the fact that three old-time families had sold their land and moved away. Nothing daunted her: insults, indifference, cruelty, frustration; she had a job to do, and, though she was growing wan-eyed and thin, she never relaxed her vigil. In only one direction did she feel she was making tangible progress: with Ira Barkley. Barkley was weakening under her insistence, her relentless pursuit. He begged her for mercy, for a few days of rest; several times she sensed that he was about to tell her something; each time he gave way to a physical collapse instead and had to be put to bed, feverish and trembling.

Then one day late in August, when Margaret felt he could not hold out against her much longer, Ira Barkley disappeared. All that Neill could tell her was that he had "gone back to where he come from, some little burg around San Diego." When she ran to Hauser's office to cry out impulsively that Barkley's flight was an admission of guilt, August caught her roughly by the arm and shouted, "You little fool, he went away because you were killing him, because his health couldn't stand your senseless attacks. Go back to Los Angeles and leave us in peace!"

And so her efforts over the long hot summer came to nothing.

In September she returned to the Alvarado Street bungalow, where Grace embraced her warmly and asked to be allowed to help in the fight. When the courts opened their fall term, Margaret prevailed upon Norman to file his bill of complaint.

"We don't dare," protested Norman. "We have nothing to go into court with."

"Please, Norm, do it for my sake. Something will turn up. I'll feel better . . . I'll be able to work better . . ."

She questioned the manager of the Bon Marché; he remembered vaguely telling somebody that Hilda Hauser had paid for her purchase with five ten-dollar bills, but could give no further information. She scraped up an acquaintance with one of the saleswomen in an attempt to secure an impression of Hilda's behavior the day she had bought her baby-blue dress. She tackled Hamilton Root's office but, finding the doors locked against her, hired a detective to get what information he could on the meetings between Root and Hauser before the trial. After two months, he submitted a report that Ira Barkley had been brought into Root's office by Hauser, where he had told Root the same story he had told in court.

When she could think of no people to see, she spent her time in Norman's office poring over lawbooks, reading cases on slander, studying recent decisions to extract material to prove that John had been unjustly convicted. When November came and the date set for the Annister hearing was close at hand, she redoubled her efforts; no clue was too slight to investigate, no lead too slender or farfetched to follow. She secured an appointment with the mayor of Los Angeles and laid the case before him; he could think of no way to help. She went to see the president of the bar association; he refused to comment on the ethics of Root's presentation of the case, telling her that John Annister should have appealed. She went back to Mission Valley for yet another week of searching and seeking . . . Norman had to ask for a postponement; the case was put over until February.

She and Grace spent the Christmas holidays with the Martells. There was even less happiness for her this year than there had been the last, with John fading in the Alvarado Street bungalow. Last year she had felt strong and confident that she could vindicate her grandfather: only hard work would be required, and undying faith. But now she had been working for seven months . . . and she was farther away from the necessary new evidence than when she had begun.

On New Year's Day she returned to Los Angeles to start on the trail again, seeking aid from every possible source, interviewing, questioning, checking facts, planning, hoping, pushing her mind out to the farthest limits of its imagination, praying for help. But once again Norman had to ask for a postponement. The new date was set for May; unless they went to trial in May their case would be thrown out.

Very little money remained of the few thousands John Annister had left but, in the ensuing three months, Margaret threw every last dollar of it into the fight, hiring investigators to find Ira Barkley, making a trip to Sacramento to see the attorney general of California and plead for his assistance, spending two days in the neighboring town of Stockton with Mary Shoemaker. When the first of May came she was exhausted.

On the afternoon before the day of the trial, she burst into Norman's office, closed the door of the small book-lined room behind her and leaned against it for support.

"Norm," she said in a strange, hushed tone, "they've found Ira Barkley. He's living in Alvista . . . near San Diego."

"But, Margaret, the hearing comes up tomorrow," he expostulated. "You worked on Ira for so many months, and he would never give you anything . . ."

She came forward, leaning across his desk with her fist clenched between her breasts.

"It's not too late yet! I've followed ten thousand other leads that looked hopeless . . . Call it a hunch, a presentiment, but I've got a sure feeling inside me that if I can get to him he'll tell me the whole story."

Norman sat twining his finger through his hair. After a few moments he jumped up, grabbed his hat off the tree behind him, came around the desk and took Margaret by the arm.

"The quicker you get there, the better."

By four o'clock she was sitting in a train in the Southern Pacific depot, waiting for it to pull out for San Diego.

"If Ira gives you anything we can use, send me a telegram," Norman told her. "I'll come down in the morning, just as soon as I can get the court to issue a commission to perpetuate testimony."

"I'll wire you tonight," she replied, kissing him

good-by. "I'll have something for us, I'm positive."

It was a torturous four-hour train ride, but at eight o'clock she reached Alvista, descended in the darkness and hired a hack driver to take her to 417 Pine Street. It proved to be a clapboard rooming house not far from the station. The big blowzy woman who answered her ring said, "Ira Barkley? Yes, he's here. But he's a mighty sick man."

"That's why I've come all the way from Los Angeles to see him."

"Then follow me upstairs. Look out you don't trip over that tear in the carpet."

Margaret followed the woman up the ill-lighted stairs. She threw open a door; Margaret entered and the door was closed behind her. In a wide brass bed lay Ira Barkley, his face on the pillow weazened almost beyond recognition. Margaret crossed and shook him by the shoulder.

"Ira Barkley," she said. "It's me, Margaret Annister."

With an almost desperate summoning of will he turned his head on the pillow. Remembrance filtered into his eyes.

"Thank God," he whispered. "Thank God you come. For days I been laying here . . . afraid to die. I been calling him . . . John Annister . . . wanting to tell him . . . so I could die in peace . . ."

Margaret caught her breath; tears flooded into her eyes and suddenly she felt weak. She drew a rattan chair up to the bed, took pencil and paper from her purse.

"Tell me everything, Ira."

". . . Hilda . . . she took the widow's money . . ." He stopped to gasp for breath. "That's why August . . . he made me . . . give envelopes . . ." He paused again to look at her through narrow slits of eyes. ". . . I made a third envelope . . . August gave me fifty dollars . . . to put in . . ."

Margaret had been getting down every word.

"Then August Hauser made you testify at the trial?"

"I was sick . . . I needed my job. . . ."

She stood over him with her pencil and paper.

"I want you to sign this, Ira."

"I'm too weak . . . I can't . . ."

She put an arm across his back and helped him to sit up.

"Ira, you must. Here, take this pencil. I'll help you."

He grasped the pencil in his emaciated hand and scrawled his name in a downward slant. Then, mustering his last bit of strength, he wrote, "August gave me fifty dollars to put in third envelope . . . Mary Shoe never took the money. . . ."

"Thank you, Ira," she said quietly, releasing him. "You've paid your debt to my grandfather."

"Thank God," his lips said, and he closed his eyes wearily.

Margaret tiptoed downstairs, asked the landlady to go up to him, then walked to the local inn, sent a telegram to Norman, rented a room and threw herself across the top of the bed.

Norman arrived at three the next afternoon with a court reporter. Margaret was watching for him in the lobby of the inn; she jumped up with a bright smile when she saw him come through the doorway.

"I've got it, Norm," she cried, thrusting the Barkley paper toward him. "A confession, and signed."

Norman licked the dust off his lips while reading the paper.

"Good!" he exclaimed when he had finished. "I've notified Hamilton Root. He's coming down on the evening train."

She stared at him uncomprehendingly.

"Hauser's lawyer? But why?"

"We have to get a deposition. The opposing attorneys have a right to be present so they can cross-examine. I have a court reporter with me; we'll get the local judge and notary to act as witnesses."

"But, Norm," she cried, "you can't."

"Why not?"

"Ira Barkley died last night."

She saw his face muscles sag.

"But we don't need him," she exclaimed, "we've got his signature . . ."

Norman swore under his breath.

"That isn't enough, not when the man who makes the confession is dead. Without a deposition the court will never set aside the sheriff's sale." He blinked his eyes hard. "Looks like August Hauser wins again," he said despondently.

Margaret put her hand on his arm and held it firmly.

"No. This time we win. I tell you, with this affidavit we win."

22

THE HEARING before the judge of the supreme court was in sharp contrast to the first trial, for the courtroom was empty of spectators and jury. Norman had his case closely organized: he went back to the night of the church social, when Hilda Hauser had appeared in her new gown, and worked forward step by step to Ira Barkley's testimony at the trial. Suddenly his voice rose, and he plunged into the story of August Hauser's subornation of perjury. When he had finished, he offered the Barkley affidavit in evidence to substantiate his claim.

Root fought the admission of the Barkley affidavit with every legal device he knew, but the judge admitted it, subject to a motion to strike it out at the end of the trial. Root then charged Margaret with trickery in staging a deathbed confession, demanded to know why he had not been informed in time to be present at a deposition, attacked the authenticity of the signature, the validity of a confession allegedly signed by a man so ill he died immediately afterward, and lastly quoted four cases showing that where no deposition had been taken, where the witness was no longer alive to corroborate the charges in the confession, the court did not have the power to set aside a sheriff's sale. He then moved that the Barkley affidavit be stricken from the record. The judge considered the motion for several moments before speaking.

"That won't be necessary," he said. "In a case of this nature, a deposition is required before new evidence can be admitted. The courts of the land have decreed an affidavit to be insufficient. Motion to set aside the sheriff's sale denied."

Norman buried his hot tired face in his hands. He had known the case would be decided this way; he had warned Margaret that it would . . . yet he felt the failure to be his fault, that he had somehow been inadequate, remiss. Then he felt Margaret's cool lips on his cheek and looked up to find her eyes glowing with excitement.

"Norm, how long will it take us to get half a dozen copies of the transcript of the record?"

"The clerk will type them up immediately, if we pay him something extra."

"Then please ask him to. I want them to take with us tonight to Mission Valley."

The people of the valley had not been told about the second trial in Los Angeles; the Beaudrys, Hubbards, Temples and Wolkskills were astonished when Margaret burst in upon them, crying, "Come along with me to the Hausers!" Norman had been dispatched to pick up Grace, his mother and father, the Lankershims and Maxwell Widney. They were assembled in the Hauser front room when Margaret arrived. She asked everyone to be seated, then took her stand before the fireplace.

"I asked you all to come here because I wanted you to know about the hearing that took place today to set aside the sheriff's sale on Mission Oaks. We went into that hearing with a signed confession from Ira Barkley telling exactly how fraud and perjury had been committed at the trial of my grandfather. We lost the case on the technical grounds that the Hauser attorney had not been able to question Barkley before he died. But the judge believed the Barkley confession to be legitimate and honest; the proof is that he admitted the affidavit into evidence. I have with me a number of copies of the transcript of the case, which I will give you to read. First I want you to see this paper, with Barkley's confession on it, and his signature."

There was a quick murmur among those assembled. August sprang up from his needlework rocker, shouting, "You can't come into my home and . . ."

"Just a moment, August Hauser," Margaret interrupted, her eyes turned up fearlessly to the man before her.

"That confession is a pack of lies . . . a fraud . . ."

"Fine! I'll give you the chance to prove it. In your office you have Ira Barkley's signature on hundreds of official papers, tax receipts and the like. Bring some of those signatures here; let these folks compare them with the signature on Barkley's confession."

"I'll do nothing of the sort," exclaimed Hauser, his face reddening. "Those papers belong to me . . ."

"On the contrary," broke in Norman, "they belong to the county."

Hauser whirled on Margaret. "The sooner you take yourself and your troublemaking out of Mission Valley . . ."

False Witness

Maxwell Widney had been standing at one of the heavily draped front windows. He came forward to the fireplace.

"Mr Hauser, you have no right to refuse those papers," he said. "If the Barkley confession will clear up this case, then I say let's clear it up and see justice done . . . no matter who has to suffer."

Hauser looked as though Widney had struck him. He stumbled to his rocker and cried weakly for water. Hilda went to her father, her pretty mask hard and grim.

"Do what they ask!" she commanded. "Can't you see we can't fight any more?"

"Please, August, please," sobbed his wife. "Make peace."

Hilda turned to Maxwell, the hardness gone from her manner.

"Maxwell, I wanted to tell the truth . . . right at the beginning when they began accusing Mary Shoe —but he wouldn't let me. Then when things got so bad and everybody was fighting about it, I was afraid to confess . . . I was afraid you wouldn't marry me . . . that I'd be hounded out of Mission Valley in disgrace, be blamed for everything that had happened. That's why I lied to you, Maxwell, when you asked me to tell the truth . . . It was because I was afraid . . ."

August made a clutching movement in the direction of his heart.

"Save yourself the trouble, Father," Hilda said coldly; "those trumped-up heart attacks won't get you anything this time. You're to blame for all this. I begged you to let me confess . . . to let me tell Maxwell . . . but all the time you were afraid for yourself . . . what it would do to your position . . . your business. I wanted to do the right thing—but you kept forcing your schemes on people, getting us in deeper and deeper—and now the responsibility for driving out Mary Shoe . . . yes, and killing John Annister . . . is on you!" She sank onto a chair in the corner of the room. "It was my father's fault I stole that money! I wanted a new dress . . . For weeks I pleaded for a few dollars . . . but he was too miserly . . . He wouldn't even give his own daughter anything . . ."

Mrs Hauser went to Hilda and held her daughter's face against her thin, aching bosom.

"Yes, August, the child is right. It's all been caused by your stinginess, your greed. Those humiliating things you made me tell John Annister . . . how I had to pinch and scrape . . . they're all true. I couldn't have told him so if it hadn't been true. I wish to God I had pinched and scraped . . . saved that fifty dollars . . ."

For a moment there was no sound in the room but August's heavy breathing and the weeping of his wife and daughter. When August looked up his eyes were covered with a film.

"What . . . what do you want of me?"

Margaret reached into her brief case.

"Sign these two affidavits. The first one declares that you know Mary Shoemaker to be innocent of the crime for which she was excommunicated; that one is to get her reinstated in the Union Church. The second admits the wrong you have done to John Annister, exonerates him from the charge of slander, and vindicates his stand on the innocence of Mary Shoemaker. I have one more paper for you to sign: it is a deed for the return of Mission Oaks to the Annister estate."

Widney brought pen and ink from the sideboard in the dining room. Hauser blindly signed his name across the bottom of the pages. Tim Temple, who had been holding a whispering conclave with the Martells, Wolkskills, Lankershims and Hubbards, came forward.

"There's one thing more we want," he announced. "Just hand us your resignation as president of the church. Then maybe we'll be able to get our people back together again."

Hauser looked up at Widney, who showed no mercy.

"Do as they ask."

Hauser wrote his name on the paper prepared and handed to him by Norman, then pushed himself upward with his arms, took a few faltering steps and pitched forward onto his face. For an almost imperceptible moment they let him lie there, then Herman picked him up and carried him to his bedroom.

"Reverend Widney," said Margaret, turning to Maxwell and speaking in a soft voice, "I am bringing my grandfather back for burial in the church cemetery on Sunday. Will you say the services over him?"

"Yes, Margaret. I will say them."

The following Sunday morning, the Mission Valley congregation stood before its white church on the hilltop. Excepting August Hauser, who lay on his bed with his right side paralyzed, every man, woman and child had come to pay homage to John Annister. While Norman Martell hammered the Annister plaque back into the front beam, the Reverend Maxwell Widney preached a short sermon extolling the beauties and virtues of the Ninth Commandment. Then he led his people to the cemetery on the crest of the knoll, where John Annister lay in a fresh grave by the side of Margarita.

"It has long been said in Mission Valley that John Annister loved good for its own sake. That is the finest tribute that can be paid to any man. The days of his years were rich with love for all of us; he gave his life to show us that, above all, we must be honest and just with our neighbors. He would ask you now to forgive your neighbors their trespasses against you, just as he would ask you to forgive yourselves your trespasses against him. . . . Let us pray."

While the congregation stood with bowed heads, the Reverend Mr Widney opened his Bible to the Twenty-third Psalm and read in a low voice:

"The Lord is my shepherd: I shall not want.

"He maketh me to lie down in green pastures: He leadeth me beside the still waters.

"He restoreth my soul; He leadeth me in the paths of righteousness for His name's sake."

The Bible closed in his hand; the minister looked over the bowed heads toward the south pass and continued:

False Witness

"Yea, though I walk through the valley of the shadow of death, I will fear no evil: for Thou art with me; Thy rod and Thy staff they comfort me. Amen."

"Amen."

The people of Mission Valley slowly turned away and went down the trail. After a time only Margaret and Norman remained behind on the crest of the hill, with the Pacific Ocean lying blue and fathomless to the west, the Sierra Madres rocky and immutable to the east, and at their feet, Mission Oaks, white and serene in its ring of trees.